Just Be Here

Just Be Here
Mainely Romance, Book 3

by Susan Page Davis

Chapter 1

Poacher Detail

Libby Sharpe turned in at the gravel driveway to the old farmhouse and noted with relief that her housemate Kim's car was in the carport. But as she eased her Toyota Tercel slowly into place behind Kim's car, she noticed the rear portion of an unfamiliar vehicle parked on the other side of the house.

Strange. Kim must have company, but the driver of the dark SUV would have had to cross the lawn to park there.

Libby gathered her purse, a tote bag, and two plastic store bags from the front seat and walked to the side door, which opened from the carport into the kitchen. The old barn that had once been connected to the farmhouse had been torn down decades earlier, and the carport was added at the side of the house. She flipped the light switch as she entered the kitchen.

"Hi!" Kim came in from the living room with a coffee mug in one hand and a sheaf of students' math papers in the other. She stepped to the sink and pulled the curtains across the window that faced the overgrown hayfield behind the house.

"Whose car is that on the far side of the house?" Libby asked.

"Oh, that's the game wardens' vehicle," Kim said.

"Game wardens? What for?"

Kim grimaced. "Somebody was out in the back field last night. They shot a deer, over near the apple trees. I called the wardens, and they're sitting out there tonight, waiting to see if the poachers come back. I told them they could park over there so anyone driving down the lane wouldn't see them."

"Will we scare the poachers away? Should we turn the lights out?" Libby glanced toward the window where the red gingham curtains covered the glass.

"Well, the shooting did happen after Stacy and I went to bed last night," Kim said. "Maybe we should turn this light out. I don't think they'd be able to see the living room light from that side."

Libby picked up her things, and Kim switched off the kitchen light. Together they walked into the small living room.

"How was your trip?"

"Great. My mom fed me too much, as usual, and I spent too much money, as usual."

Kim laughed. "I'm glad you're back. I was getting a little concerned."

"It was my first time home since I moved up here, you know, and Mom and Dad wanted me to stay for supper. It was hard to get away afterward." Libby laid down her bags and shrugged out of her light jacket. "And of course, Mom had to tell me again about all the cousins I should be visiting up here."

"How many are there?"

"A lot, but they're all out in Belgrade or Oakland. Some of them I've never met." Libby stifled a yawn. "I ought to head right to bed. I'm exhausted."

"Don't let the wardens spook you when they leave."

"How long have they been sitting out there?"

"Since about eight." Kim looked at her wristwatch. "An hour and a half. Nick said they'll stay 'til eleven or so, but if nothing happens by then, they'll give up for tonight."

"Nick?"

"You know, Nick Palmer."

"No, I don't know him. Who is he?"

Kim's blue eyes widened in surprise. "You haven't met Nick? You have his nephew in your class."

"Joey Palmer?"

"Right. Nick's his uncle. He goes to our church. You must

have seen him. He usually comes in late Sunday mornings, wearing his uniform."

"Guess I'm not very observant." Libby shook her head. "How's Stacy?"

"She's fine. I put her to bed an hour ago. She wanted to stay up and watch the deer and wait for Aunt Libby. Do you mind if she calls you that?"

"No, it's fine, as long as she remembers to call me 'Miss Sharpe' at school."

"Well, I guess we should go to sleep," Kim said. "I'll undress in the bathroom so the light from my window won't show. Yours is all right, I think."

They headed up the stairs together. "Come into my room and see the skirt I bought," Libby said. "I think I like it, but it's olive drab—not a very exciting color. Oh, and I brought Stacy a stuffed kitten, if you don't mind. I couldn't resist it."

Kim chuckled. "Isn't it great to have an excuse to buy things that you're too mature for?"

Half an hour later, Libby sank into her bed with her open Bible. She was getting used to the nighttime creaks of the old farmhouse and the quiet of the night. Before a rain, she could hear a humming from the interstate highway three miles away. Other than that, the nights were usually silent, except for an occasional car passing. Early in the morning, a logger who lived a mile down the road would take his rattling empty pulp truck out.

The general lack of noise had required an adjustment from Libby. For her first two weeks at the farmhouse, she had lain awake late every night, praying and thinking about the changes she'd made in her lifestyle.

It wasn't that she missed the noise of the suburb she had left a month earlier. She had never spent time in a place where she felt so isolated, so cut off. She had left her parents and friends behind to become independent and distance herself from bitter memories, but the quiet nights threatened to furnish brooding time.

7

***

In the state-issued Ford Explorer beside the farmhouse, Tom Hatfield stirred and glanced at Nick Palmer, who sat silently in the driver's seat.

"You cold?" Tom asked.

"I'm not warm." Nick didn't want to start the engine, but he wished he'd worn gloves.

"That Miss Richardson is something," Tom said.

"Mrs.," Nick corrected. "She's a widow."

"That right? Well, she's still pretty." Tom eyed Nick, ready to tease him about his bachelor state. Tom was happily married, and he was convinced Nick was missing something.

Nick shrugged. "She's not my type."

"What is your type?"

"I'll let you know when I find out."

Tom pushed the button on his wristwatch. "It's almost eleven o'clock. Had enough?"

"Give it another fifteen minutes."

"If we stay much longer, we'll freeze to death."

"True." Suddenly Nick was alert. A vehicle was driving slowly down the farm lane with no headlights.

"Hey!" Tom tensed beside him.

"I see it," Nick said. "Get ready!"

Chapter 2

Shows Great Potential

A gunshot and an engine starting pulled Libby to the edge of consciousness. She sat up in the darkness. An engine revved close to the house. Her heart hammered, and she threw back the blanket and tiptoed to the window.

The wardens' vehicle was pulling across the grass to the farm lane. Its headlights swung across the big field, illuminating a dark pickup truck. Near the gnarled old apple trees, she caught flashes of white as several deer leaped away toward the woods.

Kim rushed into Libby's room carrying a flashlight. "Did you hear that shot?"

"Yes. I think your heroes are chasing the poachers now."

Kim leaned on the windowsill with her, breathing fast and staring into the darkness.

"Nick said to stay in the house if anyone came around," Kim said.

Libby flashed her a glance. "Do you think they're in danger?"

"I don't know. Those men all have guns."

The SUV had moved down the farm lane and came to a stop behind the parked truck. Vehicle doors closed, and muffled shouts reached them. Libby squeezed her hands into fists and in her mind prayed frantically, *Lord, keep them safe!*

Brief flashes of light were followed by the roar of an

engine. The pickup truck lurched forward along the farm lane. The SUV moved rapidly behind it, toward the woods. The deer had long since disappeared into the trees.

"What's at the far end of the lane?" Libby asked, her heart racing.

"Nothing. It doesn't go anywhere, it kind of peters out. I think the farmer used it to tend the fields when they cut hay in the old days."

The Explorer's lights came on, illuminating the pickup as it swung in an arc across the field and turned back toward the road.

"How can they stop them?" Libby asked.

"They probably can't. But they've got a radio in the car."

The truck's speed increased as it lumbered back onto the farm lane, heading out toward the paved road, and the SUV sped along behind it.

"They're going to get away," Libby wailed.

Kim ran into the hallway and down the stairs. Libby hesitated, then grabbed her bathrobe and ran after her.

The truck was rapidly approaching the end of the lane and the paved road when she hurried out through the carport and joined Kim on the driveway. Suddenly the pickup swerved crazily and spun halfway around, then stopped broadside across the lane. The wardens' vehicle pulled up with its headlights flooding the pickup, and the two wardens leaped out, running toward the truck with their weapons in their hands.

Shouting came, but Libby couldn't make out the words.

"What happened?" Kim gasped.

"I don't know. It's like the driver lost control all of a sudden." Libby strained her eyes and ears. "Looks like the wardens are going to get them."

They stood gazing across the lawn and field for a couple of minutes, then Kim said, "I'd better go check Stacy. If she woke up, she'll be scared." She went into the house, turning lights on as she went.

Libby stayed on the driveway, watching. She thought she

could make out two men being held against the side of the pickup truck.

Kim came back out and joined her a couple of minutes later. "Stacy slept through it all."

"Look." Libby pointed toward town, along the paved road. A flashing blue light approached swiftly. Within seconds, a police car was parked at the end of the lane, and two men got out and approached the pickup truck.

"Guess they called for backup," Kim said. "Isn't this exciting?"

Libby laughed, rubbing her arms and shivering. "Sure is. I'm glad they got them. Guess we might as well go in. It's cold out here."

They went inside, but Kim put the carport light on as they went through the door.

"Do you think they'll come to the house?" Libby asked.

"I don't know."

"Well, I'm not going to meet cops in my bathrobe." Libby dashed up to her room and pulled on a pair of jeans. When she went back into the hall, Kim was emerging from her room. She had also hurriedly dressed.

"I wonder if they're still out there," Kim said as they went back downstairs.

A knock sounded on the carport door. Libby looked at Kim expectantly and whispered, "Open it."

Kim hesitated, then went over and swung the door wide. A tall young man in a green uniform and a bulletproof vest stood outside, smiling broadly.

The famous Nick Palmer, Libby surmised. She could see the resemblance to eight-year-old Joey in his dark hair and eyes. She hung back near the sink and let Kim handle the conversation.

"Thought you'd like to know the prisoners are on their way to the police station," Nick said. "Tom and I have to go in while they book them."

"Wonderful! What happened out there?" Kim asked.

11

Nick grinned. "Our secret weapon. The police department loaned us their spike mats tonight. When we saw them go down the lane, Tom and I laid the mats down before we followed them. I was hoping we could chase those guys into them, and it worked."

"I'm impressed. Hey, Nick, do you want some cookies?" Kim grabbed a tin from the countertop and took it to the door.

"No, that's all right. Sorry if we woke you up with all the commotion."

"Here." Kim put the cookie tin in his hands. "Share them with your partner."

"Thanks." Nick turned and went back to his Explorer.

Kim waved then closed the door and locked it. "Well, how about that?"

Libby nodded in satisfaction. "Nice ending."

"So what do you think about Nick?" Kim asked.

Libby considered. "Creative," she said. "Like his nephew. Shows great potential."

Chapter 3

And He's Polite

On Sunday morning, Libby was awakened by Stacy, who ran into her bedroom in her fuzzy pink pajamas and catapulted onto the bed shouting, "Aunt Libby! Aunt Libby! You're home!"

Libby rolled over, smiling, and gave the little girl a hug.

"I'm so glad to see you, Stacy. I missed you yesterday. What did you do all day?"

"Mommy and I did laundry and went shopping, and we talked to Mr. Palmer."

"Mr. Palmer? Oh, the game warden."

"Right. She called him and told him there were bad guys at our house the other night."

"That was scary for you." Libby watched Stacy's face carefully.

Her blue eyes grave, Stacy nodded vigorously, setting her light brown curls bouncing. "I didn't see them, but Mommy did. I was asleep. But Mommy said they were trying to catch our deer."

Libby smiled. She knew Stacy loved seeing the animals come timidly out of the woods into the field at twilight. Several times Kim had pointed out the deer to her daughter, and they had all watched them with quiet delight.

"That's right," Libby agreed. "And Mr. Palmer and his friends caught those bad guys last night."

"I know, I know!" Stacy bounced up and down, making the whole bed undulate.

Libby sat up and stretched to reach her housecoat.

"Mommy's making oatmeal," Stacy said. "Come on!"

***

Libby looked around during the opening to the church service, trying to spot some of her students and their families. They were only four weeks into the school year at Faith Christian Academy, which was attached to the church.

On the coming Friday night, the school would host an open house, and Libby would meet many of the parents. At least half the children were from families that attended other churches, but several were members at the school's affiliate church. She had met many of the parishioners, but she was still sorting out the names and trying to match children to their parents.

She located Joey Palmer, his parents and two sisters. Joey's dark hair stood up in a cowlick at the back of his head, not unlike his father's. He was one of the more active boys in Libby's combined third and fourth grade classroom. His sister Rachel was in first grade, and their father held little Amy in his arms during the opening hymn. The girls' hair was a shade lighter than Joey's, like their mother's.

Beyond them was an older couple, and Rachel Palmer tugged at the woman's sleeve and whispered in her ear. Libby decided that the couple must be her grandparents.

Ashley and April Mitchell were hard not to notice. The third-grade twins never dressed alike but called attention to themselves in every other way possible. They never sat still, and inevitably squirmed through church, whispering until their mother fixed them with a disapproving glare. Their chestnut hair was cut chin-length, and their brown eyes darted inquisitive gazes here and there.

The pair had baffled Libby for nearly two weeks in the

classroom, until she had learned to differentiate them by their teeth. April had a slight gap between her two front teeth, but Ashley didn't. She was thankful they were happy little girls. If they refused to smile, she wouldn't know who was who.

After the opening hymn, welcome, prayer, and announcements, the ushers began to take the offering, and Libby slipped her weekly tithe check from her purse.

Before the ushers reached the row where she and Kim sat with Stacy between them, Nick Palmer walked quietly in from the entry and sat down on the end of the pew. Wearing his uniform, he had a handgun in a black leather holster at his hip, and a Maine Department of Inland Fisheries and Wildlife patch on his sleeve. His badge and whistle cord gleamed on the left side of his shirt front.

The glimpse she'd had the night before hadn't given her a true picture, Libby admitted to herself. In her foggy state after being ripped from sleep, she'd seen him as half superhero and half a more mature counterpart of young Joey. Nick was very good looking in daylight, and he seemed to radiate competence and authority.

He opened his wallet and took some bills out. Libby looked away and tried not to let her glance go toward him when she laid her check in the offering plate.

She tried to focus on Pastor Wilson, a man of forty whose preaching revealed long hours of study in God's Word. He was different from her old pastor in Westbrook. Rev. Carter had been older, over sixty, and a very gentle man. His strength had been caring for his people, and his tender heart was much appreciated by the congregation.

Pastor Wilson, on the other hand, had three children still at home and one in college. He took an active part in the school's administration and led chapel for the students every day. While he loved his people, he delegated much of the visitation to his deacons and spent much time in his study at the church. His sermons were powerful, yet he stepped behind the pulpit with humility.

At the end of the service, Pastor Wilson walked down the aisle to the back of the auditorium and into the foyer, to greet people as they left. Nick stepped into the aisle but waited. Libby picked up her Bible and purse and started out along the pew, with Stacy behind her.

"Ma'am," Nick said.

Libby smiled involuntarily. So polite! If only his mischievous nephew had such good manners.

"Hello." She looked him briefly in the eye. He had the same rebellious dark hair that Joey and his father had, rich brown eyes, and dark eyebrows that arched slightly, not quite meeting over a straight nose.

As she entered the aisle, Kim came within earshot, and Nick said, "Mrs. Richardson, may I speak to you?"

"Certainly," Kim said.

Libby walked to the back of the church and waited, watching the conversation from a distance. Stacy hung on to her mother's hand, her eyes riveted on Nick's gun. People flowed past Libby, out the double door into the entry.

Kim began walking slowly toward the door with the movement of the crowd, and Nick walked beside her, continuing to speak to her.

When they were beyond the last pew, Kim glanced at Libby, stepped toward her, out of the traffic, and released Stacy's hand. Stacy flew to Libby, crying, "Is it lunch time, Aunt Libby?"

Kim nodded at what Nick was saying, but she turned toward Libby slightly and said, "Nick, I'd like you to meet my housemate. I didn't introduce you last night. Too excited, I guess. This is Libby Sharpe. Libby, this is Nick Palmer."

"Hi." Nick held out his hand, and Libby took it. He shook her hand firmly, but not too hard. "You must be the new teacher."

"Yes, I have Joey in my class," Libby said.

He nodded. "I heard."

Libby laughed self-consciously. "What did you hear?"

"I was over to my brother's Friday night, and Joey was telling me some tales." Nick smiled.

Oh, great, Libby thought. She forced herself to remain upbeat. "Nothing too outrageous, I hope."

"I think he's enjoying school this year," Nick said.

"Well, thanks for the update, Nick," said Kim. "If you need an official statement or anything, you know where to find me."

"I think we're all set. And thanks again for the tip. We've tried to catch those two for a long time. I think they've been taking a lot of deer out of season in this area." He nodded in Libby's general direction without making eye contact and moved toward the church door.

She watched him go. No doubt about it, he was appealing with his dark good looks and his reserved, boyish manners. She wondered how deep Kim's interest went. Stacy tugged at her hand, and Libby turned back toward her.

"I'm hungry," Stacy said.

Kim gazed at her with her eyebrows raised expectantly. "Well?"

"Well, he's polite." Libby felt her face reddening a bit.

Kim laughed. "Come on, let's go feed this starving child."

***

Nick left the church and went quickly to his state vehicle. Yes, he could see why Joey was exhibiting the classic signs of a crush on his third-grade teacher. That long, thick chestnut braid made her look young, too young to be a teacher. But it was her eyes that had arrested his attention. Lively, interested, but wary, too. She had stood aside while he talked to Kim, not pushing herself into the conversation, but he'd still been conscious that she watched him.

He mulled over Tom's question of the night before: what *was* his type of woman? He'd thought he knew once, but he'd realigned the criteria since then.

17

Libby Sharpe was worth investigating, if he could get past the panic that assailed him when it came to meeting new women. His heart had pounded even when he'd spoken to Kim Richardson, and she'd been a member of his church for a year. It wasn't that he was personally attracted to Kim. He'd heard her story and respected her, but he didn't think she was the right woman for him.

But was Libby Sharpe his type? Unfortunately, there was only one way to find out, and that involved the painful process of getting acquainted.

Chapter 4

On the Other Hand

Kim and Libby sat in the living room late that afternoon, reading student papers. Stacy played on the rug with plastic blocks, and Libby read through several student compositions for Kim, marking spelling and punctuation errors. Kim would give the papers a second reading for content.

"Thanks so much for doing this," Kim said.

"No problem. You've got some pretty good writers in seventh grade this year."

"I sure have. Of course, there are some pretty poor ones too."

Libby circled a spelling error.

"So, what did you really think of Nick?" Kim asked.

Libby brushed her dark hair back. "I don't know. I didn't really see him long enough to form an impression."

Kim chewed the end of her pen. "You know he's single?"

"No, I didn't know." It hadn't been specifically spelled out for her, but she'd gathered from Kim's attitude that he must be available.

"Well, he is."

Libby laid down the composition she had been reading and reached for another. "Are you interested in him?" she asked casually.

"Me? No, I'm not interested in anybody right now," Kim said. "I don't think I'm ready for that yet."

Libby looked at her friend. "I thought maybe you were. I'm sorry. It seemed important to you to know what I thought of him."

"It is, sort of. He's a nice guy. I thought maybe … you know. Maybe he'd be good for you."

Libby shifted in her armchair and looked at the title of the composition, "Memory Lapse." She said carefully, "I'm not sure I'm ready for that, either."

"Oh. I'm sorry." Kim stacked the papers she'd been working on. "I've always been a matchmaker, but I'll try to repress the tendency, if that's what you want."

Libby shrugged. "Maybe, after a while, I'll be ready to think about seeing someone again. I had sort of a bad experience last spring."

"I didn't mean to pry."

"No, it's okay." Libby gave her a rueful smile. She and Kim had only known each other a few weeks. "I just—well, it's still pretty painful. I was engaged." She sighed, looked again at the paper, and laid it aside. One of the reasons she had left Westbrook was so she wouldn't have to talk about it, and therefore, she hoped, wouldn't think about it so much.

"Had you set the date?" Kim asked timidly.

"Set the date, booked the church, the caterer, the photographer, everything. My wedding dress is at my mother's, hanging in the closet."

"So … what happened? If you don't mind my asking. And if you do, that's okay, we'll just get some ice cream and forget about it."

Libby looked into Kim's blue eyes and saw concern there. She valued Kim's friendship and felt she could safely confide her sorrow and humiliation. "Three weeks before the wedding, he told me he was having doubts. Three weeks." She shook her head. "He didn't tell me then, but he'd met somebody else."

"Crummy."

"Oh, I don't know," Libby shrugged. "It was better than having him go through with it and have the doubts after."

"Well, sure." Kim was quiet for a minute, watching Stacy build a garage with the blocks for her toy police car. "Let's get the ice cream," she said conspiratorially.

"Right."

"Come on, Stace, ice cream," Kim said.

"Oh boy!" Stacy went joyfully with them to the kitchen, where Kim generously dipped coffee ice cream into three bowls and poured chocolate syrup over it.

"I think this had better be my supper," Libby said, getting the spoons from a drawer.

"Then you'd better throw some protein on it." Kim opened a cupboard and took out a can of peanuts.

Libby laughed. "Why aren't you fat as a pig?" Her housemate was tall, five feet eight inches, but slender.

"Because I never eat when I'm alone," Kim said.

"I've never heard that one."

"Oh, it's true. That's when you gain weight. When you have people around, it helps you be moderate."

Libby considered, taking a spoonful of ice cream. "You may have something there."

"Sure, that's why I needed a roommate." Kim grinned. "Kids don't count."

"So if I never eat when I'm alone, I'll never gain weight," Libby mused.

"Absolutely. You're such a loner, you'd probably disappear." Kim turned sober. "I used to eat all the time after Eric died. I gained about twenty pounds."

"Really? You must have been depressed."

"You have no idea." Kim licked her spoon. "I was beyond depressed. Way beyond."

"Mommy, can I have whipped cream?" Stacy asked.

Kim rolled her eyes and opened the freezer for whipped topping.

"I'm sorry, Kim. Sorry you had to go through that," Libby said quietly.

Kim shrugged, scooping the whipped topping onto her

daughter's ice cream. "Well, I'm not entirely through it. It was so unexpected. Everything was going great, just like we'd planned. We were *so* happy."

Libby nodded in sympathy.

Kim's eyes focused beyond Libby, at something outside the kitchen, far in the past. "The power went out that day. I was cooking supper. Eric was supposed to be home any minute, and the power went out. I didn't know—" she sniffed a little.

Libby got up and went to the counter and came back to the table with a box of tissues. Kim took one and wiped her eyes. "Sorry."

"It's okay," Libby said.

"I didn't know it was his accident. He took out the power pole at the end of our street. A kid had ridden right out in front of him on a bicycle, and he swerved, trying not to hit him." Tears rolled down Kim's cheeks, and she wiped them away. "All I could think of was, I couldn't have his supper ready because the electricity was off."

Libby put her arms around her roommate, and Kim collapsed against her and sobbed. Libby held her, rubbing her shoulders and praying silently. After a moment Kim sat up and took another tissue.

Stacy went to her mother and patted her arm. "It's okay, Mommy. Don't cry."

Kim smiled and gave Stacy a squeeze. She looked up at Libby. "It's a lot better now, but it still hurts. I'm just getting now so I can think about him without going completely to pieces."

"How long has it been?" Libby asked.

"Two years. The first year was really bad. I took Stacy and went home to live with my parents. I was a total basket case. Couldn't do anything the first few months."

Libby nodded in sympathy.

"Then I started looking for a job, but I didn't want to put Stacy in daycare," Kim said. "Eric and I had talked about it. I was going to stay home and home school. That's why, when they offered me this, at FCA, I jumped at it. Stacy was four then, and they said she could go into the preschool class. We'd be in the same building all day. I really felt like God had arranged that for me."

"I'm sure He did," Libby said.

Kim nodded, wiping her eyes again. "Me, too. I came here and found this house to rent, and I figured it was time to start making a new life for Stacy and me."

"You're doing fine." Libby squeezed Kim's shoulders.

"Well, thanks. But, as you can see, I'm a long way from being ready for a new relationship."

"Take your time."

Kim nodded soberly. "You, on the other hand …"

"Oh, no, let's not get into that," Libby said, pulling away.

"Okay, we won't. Not today." Kim looked speculatively at her. "But you're bound to see Nick at church again."

Libby shook her head. "I told you, I'm not interested."

"I hear you." Kim was still smiling.

Chapter 5

Intriguing, Maybe

At school all week Libby worked diligently, guiding her students in preparing portfolios of their best work to leave on their desks Friday. Their parents would be coming in to talk to the teachers and would want to see samples of their children's work.

Her eight fourth-graders and twelve third-graders were bundles of energy. In the chilly fall weather, it stayed cold until the sun got high. The children arrived at school each morning with red cheeks and cold hands, but full of bounce and ready to plunge into whatever Miss Sharpe had planned for them.

Libby taught them all their subjects except Bible and music. She tried to tie their assignments together with a theme. In September she had used a transportation theme, and that had gone over well with the boys. She had covered the classroom walls with trucks, airplanes, boats, tractors and a long freight train, each child's name on one car of the train. They had studied wheels and energy in science, and they took a field trip to the Cole Land Transportation Museum in Bangor.

Now they were immersed in an autumn theme, and she found stories and poems about fall and hunting and harvest. The children made classroom decorations, autumn leaves and pumpkins cut from construction paper. Libby culled the students' seatwork for a neat paper from each, to be mounted on colorful backgrounds and hung on the bulletin board.

Parents filled the chairs in the gymnasium on Friday evening, and Pastor Wilson addressed them cordially, welcoming them and encouraging them to visit with their children's teachers and examine the students' work. He introduced the new faculty. Mr. Mills taught science and Spanish in the high school, and Miss Sharpe presided over the third- and fourth-grade classroom. Libby stood up when she was introduced and tried not to blush as the parents stared at her and Ken Mills, but it was a lost battle.

As soon as Pastor Wilson excused the group, she hurried to her classroom and stood just inside the door, ready to welcome parents.

"I'm so glad to meet you," she said over and over, and "Your daughter's desk is right over there."

She spent an hour and a half on her feet, trying always to be cordial, helpful, nonjudgmental, enthusiastic—so many things to so many people.

It was grueling, yet easier than parent nights had been at the public school where she had previously taught. Most of the parents here were Christians, and they seemed less critical than those she had met at the public school. She no longer felt they disdained her as a novice, too young, fresh out of college.

They were all anxious to see their children succeed. The mothers listened eagerly as she explained some of the projects the class had done and accepted the handout she had made of suggested read-aloud books for them to share at home with the children. The fathers scrutinized the papers on the bulletin board, each searching for the one representing their child's work.

Mr. and Mrs. Palmer came in together.

"We've met at church," Jill Palmer said. "I'm Joey's mother. This is my husband, Mike."

"Yes, hello." Libby shook their hands and pulled her eyes away from Mike Palmer's face. His brown eyes and fluffy dark hair were incredibly like Nick's, but he was a little heavier than his brother, and his smile seemed to come more easily.

"Joey is a treasure," Libby said sincerely. "I'm really glad he's in my room this year."

She showed them the portfolio the boy had labored over, spotlighting a cartoon strip Joey had drawn in art period the week before.

"Look, it's us!" Gleefully, Jill held up the strip Joey had taped together. "There's Rachel with her booboo when she fell off the swing!"

Mike took the comic strip and read it, smiling and nodding, then grinned as he reached the end. "Some kid, huh?"

"I think he shows great potential," Libby agreed. "He's creative, and he has terrific verbal skills. Math is not his favorite subject, though."

"Is he doing okay?" Mike asked.

"Yes, not too badly. I have to prod him a little."

"That doesn't surprise me," Jill said. "I have to prod him at home to clean up his room."

"It wouldn't hurt to make some flash cards of the multiplication facts and drill him a little every night," Libby suggested. "Not long, just a couple of minutes. When it comes to math, there's no substitute for drill."

"Sure, I could do that," Jill agreed.

"I'll do it when I get home every night," Mike offered.

"He'd really like it more if you did it," Jill said. She asked Libby, "Did I hear that you're living with Mrs. Richardson?"

"Yes, Kim took me on as a housemate. I enjoy being with her and Stacy."

"That's terrific," Jill said. "I hated to see her living alone. I mean, women have to be careful."

Libby nodded. "Thanks for your concern. I think it's a good arrangement for both of us."

Mrs. Mitchell, the twins' mother, claimed Libby's attention, and she drew a deep breath, switching gears mentally to Ashley and April. Nothing had been said about Nick Palmer. But then, why should it?

***

Libby didn't see Nick at church the next Sunday until they were leaving the building. He was waiting at the bottom of the steps, leaning against the railing, holding his hat. With a jolt, she realized she'd been hoping to see him. The morning had seemed the teeniest bit flat until that moment.

"Well, hello. Didn't think you were here," Kim greeted him.

He smiled. "I snuck in late, as usual."

"So, what's the word on the poachers?"

"They made bail, but we'll see them in court soon." Nick looked past Kim at Libby, then away. "They had two loaded rifles and a spotlight, and they'd fired at a buck just before we swooped down on them. I think these guys are going to do some time. They've both got priors. Thanks again for calling us when you did."

"Glad to do it," Kim said. She glanced around at Libby, who stood behind her.

Libby wished she could say something witty or profound, but nothing came to mind, so she decided she was better off keeping her mouth closed.

"Mr. Palmer, did you get the bad guys?" Stacy asked, reaching for Nick's hand and pulling herself up on tiptoe to look at his face more closely.

He bent toward her. "We sure did, pumpkin."

Stacy rewarded him with a wide smile.

"Would you like to eat lunch with us?" Kim asked.

"Oh, no, thanks, this was my lunch," Nick said.

"What, church?"

"Yeah, I took my lunch hour so I could come here."

"So that's why you come in late every Sunday."

"You found me out. I've got a sandwich in the car." He looked at his watch. "Gotta get going now. See you." He put on his hat and tipped the brim just a bit, in salute to Kim and Stacy, then nodded solemnly at Libby. "Miss Sharpe," he said quietly, and turned toward the parking lot.

"He's cute," Kim said dispassionately, taking Stacy's hand and walking with her and Libby toward the car.

"Not the word I would have used," Libby mused.

"Oh? What word would you have used?"

Libby stopped beside her Toyota and watched the black Explorer with 'Inland Fisheries and Wildlife' and the state seal on the door as it crept across the parking lot and rolled into the street.

"Intriguing, maybe?" she said at last.

Kim smiled. "That's progress."

Chapter 6

Telling You Once

Nick headed south. A complaint had come by radio of teenagers driving all-terrain vehicles along the railroad tracks near the former site of the old depot in North Belgrade. No doubt they would be gone before he arrived on the scene. He was authorized to enforce traffic laws for all types of vehicles, but mostly he monitored boats, snowmobiles and ATVs.

As he cruised along Route 11, he hardly saw the splashes of color in the hardwoods beside the road. The leaves were turning fast now, and green had given way to scarlet, gold, orange, and amber. His thoughts were back at the church, where Libby Sharpe had stood so silent and grave.

He'd wanted to speak to her. He ought to be glad Kim Richardson was friendly. If she hadn't stopped to chat with him, Libby would probably have walked by him without a glance. On the other hand, if Kim hadn't been there, ready to converse, he might have gotten up the nerve to say hello to Libby.

Her hair had hung loose down her back that morning, a sheet of deep chestnut. He had sat two rows behind her, coming in just after the choir sang. She bent her head over her Bible. Once or twice she had leaned toward Stacy to hear the little girl's whisper, and he had seen her profile. It was a good seat, if you wanted to observe a demure, beautiful woman. Not so good if you wanted to concentrate on the sermon.

He almost missed the turn at Station Road but pulled his thoughts back to the present just in time. He drove to the end of it, near Messalonskee Lake. No ATVs in sight, as he had expected. He drove down a camp road as far as a large family campground, deserted now that the summer season was over.

Three four-wheelers came tearing around the office building, straight into his path. Nick hit the brake, and at the same time flipped the switch activating his blue light.

The boys stopped their vehicles, the first within inches of his Explorer's front bumper. The passenger flew forward, shoving the driver up on the handlebars.

Nick got out of the Explorer and walked toward them, trying to look large and official. The six high school boys would be enough to overpower him if they dared.

"Afternoon, boys. What's up?"

"Nothing," said the driver of the first ATV. He smiled, an open, innocent look. His passenger straightened up and rubbed his nose.

"This is private property," Nick said. The six boys stared balefully at him, and he made eye contact with each in turn.

"We're not doing nothing," one offered. He sat on the back of the second ATV.

Nick looked them over slowly. They fidgeted a little. All wore headgear. That was in their favor.

"Give me your names, please." He took his notebook from his pocket.

The first boy hesitated, then answered, and the others followed his lead.

"Are we in trouble?" the first boy, Larry Shibles, asked. "My dad said we could ride down here. I didn't know we weren't supposed to."

"Well, you've all got helmets, so I'm going to be nice today," Nick said. "I'm telling you this once. You can't come down here to the campground. You're trespassing. If I get a call from somebody saying you're on private property with those things again, I won't be so nice, got it?"

They all nodded solemnly.

"And another thing."

Their attention didn't waver. Nick closed the notebook and put it back in his shirt pocket. "If you take an ATV on the railroad track or on a public roadway, that's a fifty-dollar fine the first time, you understand?"

Again they nodded uneasily.

"Now, can you get home without going on a public way?"

They looked at each other.

"We'll have to cross a couple of roads and maybe go a little ways on the side of the road," Larry said at last.

"All right, you do that. Go straight across the roads when you have to, and watch carefully for traffic. And don't you be riding on the road. Because the next time you do, you'll get a ticket."

The boys nodded sheepishly.

"All right, let's see your registrations."

The three drivers pulled out the paperwork, and he scrutinized each in turn.

"Okay, this one runs out this month," Nick said to the boy driving the third vehicle. "Don't forget to register it, will you?"

The young man shook his head.

"All right, get out of here, and be careful."

The three ATV's started off up the dirt road, and Nick turned his Explorer around and followed them slowly. When he was nearly to the paved road, he picked up his radio microphone and called the dispatcher.

"The ATV situation is handled."

"10-4, there's a complaint of dogs running deer on the Townfarm Road in Sidney," came the dispatcher's impersonal voice.

"I'll be there in twenty minutes."

Chapter 7

Riding Together

Stacy grew more and more excited as the week went by. Her mother was planning a visit to her grandparents' house for the weekend, and the little girl could hardly wait. The trip would take close to four hours each way, and they would leave right after school on Friday.

"What are your plans for the weekend, Libby?" Kim asked on the way to school Thursday morning.

"I'm not sure. I might drive down and see my folks Saturday. And I was thinking about that concert Pastor Wilson announced at prayer meeting last night."

"Where is it?" Kim asked. "Bangor?"

"Yes, tomorrow night, and it sounds really good. A string quartet from a Christian college."

"You want to drive an hour by yourself to hear it?"

"I think there's going to be carpooling from the church," Libby said. "Maybe I can get someone to ride with me."

When school ended on Friday, the three of them rushed home, and Libby helped pack Kim' and Stacy's luggage into the car. Stacy came to her for a hug.

"I hope you have a great visit with your Nana and Grandpa," Libby said. She stood watching as Kim drove away.

She went in the house and got a container of yogurt from the refrigerator, then rifled the tote bag she carried to church for Sunday's bulletin. Carpooling for the concert would leave the church at six o'clock.

After putting a load of laundry in the washer, she went over her lesson plans for the next week. She changed into a fresh dress, wearing wool for the first time that season in deference to the chill predicted for the evening. At quarter to six she was sitting in her car in the church parking lot.

She waited. At five minutes to six, she wondered if she had the right night. No other cars had joined hers. At two minutes to six, a gray Dodge Ram pickup pulled in. It rolled slowly across the lot and into the parking spot next to hers. The driver's door opened and Nick Palmer got out and slowly approached her door. Libby rolled down her window.

"Hi," he said somberly.

"Hi."

He was wearing a brown corduroy sport jacket, a green shirt, and a striped tie. Libby had never seen him out of uniform. He was no less dashing in his civilian clothes.

"You going to the concert?" he asked cautiously.

She bit her lip. "I was planning to. "Guess not many people are going."

Nick looked around.

"Here comes Pastor." Relief filled his voice.

Libby opened her door and got out of the car as Nick turned to greet Pastor Wilson.

"Hello, folks," the pastor said cheerfully. "Is this it? Big turnout."

"I guess so," Nick said.

"Well, Sarah and I were going to go, but I've just had a call, and I need to go to the hospital," Pastor Wilson said. "Mrs. Caswell fell and broke her hip, and the family wants me to go, so I guess we'll miss the concert."

"That's too bad." Nick sounded genuinely concerned.

"Well, keep her in prayer." The pastor looked from Nick to Libby and back. "You two all right with going together? If not, maybe my wife would ride along, but she was going to go to the hospital with me."

"It's okay," said Nick.

Libby swallowed but said nothing. She hadn't considered that she might actually be riding with Nick.

"All right, enjoy," said the pastor, and he walked away toward the parsonage.

Nick turned slowly toward her. "Do you want … to ride with me?"

Libby hesitated. "I—do you want me to? Because I don't have to go. It was just something to do. Kim's away, and I thought it would be nice…" She stopped, feeling she'd talked for hours.

Nick looked up at the steeple. "You got a coat?"

"Y-yes." She realized then that the wind was cutting through her blue wool dress.

Nick seemed to come to a decision and faced her squarely. "Come on, then. Bring your stuff."

Libby found herself trembling as she opened the car door and retrieved her jacket and purse. She wasn't at all sure Nick was happy with the situation, or that she was either. She put on her jacket, flipping her braid out over the collar.

He opened the passenger door of the truck for her and put his hand on her arm, giving her a little leverage as she climbed up.

"The seat belt's here." He pulled it part way out for her.

She took it from him and found herself looking into his eyes, six inches away. It was a bit unnerving to be so close to him, and to realize she was about to be confined with him in the truck for an hour.

"Look, you don't have to take me," she said.

"Well, I want to go. You do, don't you?" he backed off a few inches with a slightly confused air.

"Well, yes, but … I wasn't sure you wanted to go with me." There. It was in the open.

His eyes questioned her. He glanced across the parking lot, then back at her. "Look, I'd be happy to take you, okay?"

She nodded slowly.

His tentative smile came out, and she found herself smiling back.

He closed the door, went around the truck, got in, and buckled his seat belt without saying anything. He drove to the interstate and onto the entrance ramp. Libby held her purse carefully on her lap. When they had gone about five miles north, he looked her way and said, "Need more heat?"

"Maybe a little."

He switched the heater a notch higher and smiled her way, then turned his eyes back to the road ahead. "You sure talk a lot."

She laughed, and they looked at each other.

I need to say something. She cast about for a topic. His work? His nephew, Joey? Church?

Chapter 8

One Thing in Common

"So, do you like being a warden?" Libby ventured.

"Yup."

She smiled. No more yes-or-no questions. "What's the best thing about it?"

Nick stared ahead for a moment, then said, "Being outside a lot, I guess. I get out on the lakes a lot in summer, and this time of year we check hunters. We had moose season this week, and it's bird season now. I love fall."

"You like to hunt?" she asked.

"When I have time."

"What do you do in the winter?"

"Oh, there's ice fishing and snowmobilers, a lot of stuff like that. Trappers to check on." He glanced across at her. "You from around here?"

"I grew up in Westbrook. Just moved up here in late August. I have some aunts and uncles and a bunch of cousins in Kennebec County, but I don't know them very well. Most of them are Cooks."

"Oh, you're related to the Cooks?"

"Yes."

"The ones with President names?"

She laughed. "Yes, my great-grandfather was George Washington Cook, and my grandmother was his daughter, Abigail Cook. Her brothers were John Adams Cook and

Thomas Jefferson Cook. But she married a Sharpe, so my name's Sharpe."

"Okay. And you moved up here to teach?"

"That's right."

Nick drove in silence for at least two miles before he said, "So, is this your first year teaching?"

"No," Libby said, "I taught for two years in Gorham, in a public school."

"Like it?"

"Not really. I liked some things about it, but the kids are hard, even in fifth grade. That's what I taught there. They're already mouthy at that stage." She shook her head. She'd really wanted to like those kids, but only a few had let her in through their shells.

"So, you didn't want to teach public school anymore?"

Libby pulled in a breath. She didn't really want to tell him her most intimate secrets yet. "I ... wanted a change. Wanted something different." It sounded lame.

"Do you like this better?" he asked.

"Yes, I do. It's early yet, but I like it. It's a much smaller school, and I have two grades in my room, but it's all right. And the people are much nicer here. It's great to be working with Christians."

"Tom Hatfield, the guy that was with me last week ..." He looked her way, and she nodded. "He's not a Christian. Lives over in Unity. I work with him once in a while. He thinks I'm nuts."

"Really?"

"Yup." Nick laughed a little. "I tried to talk to him about spiritual things the first few times we rode together, and he told me not to preach at him. Now I just tell him he knows what I think, and if he ever wants to talk about it to tell me."

"Does he ever tell you?"

"Not yet." He drove without speaking for several minutes.

"So why did you decide to come tonight?" Libby asked.

He looked at her blankly, then back at the road. "Well, it's music. I like good music."

"Of course." She was silenced.

Three miles later, he said, "You like music?"

"Yes. Classical, mostly. And sacred music. I figured a string quartet would play a little classical."

"Me, too. Wish I'd learned to play the violin," Nick said.

"Really? Did you play any instruments?"

"I took trumpet in school. They didn't have an orchestra, just band."

"I took piano for three years," Libby said. "Then my teacher quit."

He laughed. "Not because of you, I hope."

"No, she got married and moved away. But my folks never found me another teacher, and I got interested in other things."

"So, you plan to teach all your life?"

"What kind of question is that?" She eyed him archly.

"I dunno. I mean, is it a career for you? Do you like it well enough?"

"Maybe, if I have to."

"Doesn't sound like you're that thrilled with the prospect."

"Well, I used to think I wanted to be a veterinarian."

"No kidding. Why didn't you?"

She sighed. "First I found out you had to take six semesters of chemistry in pre-vet, and I didn't do so well in chemistry in high school. And the cost—graduate school and all. My parents couldn't handle it. The competition for vet schools is really fierce too. I just didn't think I'd make it all the way through."

He didn't say anything.

"Then I decided to become a lawyer."

He laughed outright. "A lawyer? That's easier than being a vet?"

"Maybe not easier than *being* a vet, but maybe *becoming* a lawyer is easier than becoming a vet. Maybe. For some people." *Calm down. You sound defensive.* "But it still meant grad school and big bucks, so I didn't get to find out how hard it was really going to be."

"So you teach."

"Right."

He shook his head. "You really don't sound happy to me."

"Well, please don't tell my students or their parents." Should she be offended? She didn't think Nick should pass judgment on her happiness or lack of it after a total of five minutes' conversation. "I try to be a good teacher. I really work hard at it. At trying to like it and getting my kids to like learning."

"I guess that's what it comes down to," he said thoughtfully. "Some people are good at it without trying very hard."

She didn't know whether to feel insulted or not. He obviously didn't think very highly of her, which was a disappointment. The more she learned about him, the more she liked him, but he seemed to find her both too melancholy and unsuited for her job. She said nothing, but gazed out the window, watching the bright yellows and oranges of the hardwoods deepen to browns and blacks as the sun lowered behind them.

Fifteen minutes later, he exited the highway and drove a short distance to the church hosting the concert.

"Mike says Joey really likes having you for a teacher, if it's any consolation," Nick said as he turned in at the parking lot.

"I like Joey."

"Jill says he's reading more at home. You loaned him some books or something."

"Joey told me he likes airplanes, so I took him a couple of books I enjoyed as a kid. Flying adventures."

He shut off the engine and looked at the church. A stream of people was going in at the front door.

"We're here. You ready?"

"Guess so."

He opened his door, and she opened hers and climbed

down. They went in together. The auditorium was filling from the back, and they found seats two thirds of the way forward.

Libby decided to forget about Nick Palmer for an hour and just soak up the music. The musicians were very talented, and she was satisfied that it had been worth the drive. There was no preaching, but the student musicians gave short testimonies between the musical selections, and offering plates were passed. She contributed five dollars and forced herself not to see how much Nick put in.

As the music filled the air, she was almost able to ignore him. Then he leaned over between numbers and said in her ear, "That first violinist is really good."

She nodded. Nick's shoulder was touching hers. Amazing how it affected her, through layers of wool, corduroy and cotton. She shifted slightly so that he wasn't touching her anymore, but it was harder to ignore him after that.

She found herself turning her head just a little to glimpse his profile when the violinist completed a particularly brilliant passage. He was rapt. As the last note faded away, he smiled and glanced at her. She smiled just a little, and he nodded, settling back in the pew, contented.

Well, they had one thing in common, at least. Libby dearly loved good music. And she liked nature and the outdoors, too, although she had never had a chance to really rough it or ramble through the countryside. And they shared their faith. She wondered if all of that was enough.

Chapter 9

Again on Purpose

When it was over, they made their way slowly out with the crowd and found the truck. Frost had formed on the windshield, and Nick quickly unlocked Libby's door then got in the driver's seat, started the engine, and turned on the defroster.

"I was wondering," he said, watching the frost slowly recede from the glass.

She looked at him expectantly.

He turned to face her. "I was wondering ..."

"What?"

Still he hesitated. "Don't get mad, now."

"I won't." He probably was wondering why she thought she could be an adequate teacher.

"Okay ... I was wondering if we could get a milkshake or something?"

Libby was just short of stunned. Prolonging their time together was the last request she had expected. And milkshakes, in October. "Too cold for that."

"Oh." He moved the gearshift into reverse.

She felt she had made a gaffe. What harm would it do to spend a few more minutes with him? He didn't hold her in total derision, or he wouldn't have asked her. If she totally repulsed him tonight, she would always regret it and wonder if he might not have found one little thing to like about her, if she'd just given him the chance.

"Hot cocoa, maybe," she said.

"Okay." He was smiling. She saw it in the lights from the car behind them.

He drove toward the highway and pulled in at a McDonald's. A school bus sat in the parking lot and they could see about forty students through the restaurant's windows.

"They're probably on the way home from a football game," Libby hazarded.

"Maybe we don't want to go in."

"Maybe not."

He drove through the drive-up lane, ordered two hot chocolates, and collected them on the other side of the building, then found a spot to park under a streetlamp.

"I really enjoyed the music." Libby carefully peeled the lid from her cup.

"Me, too." Nick blew on his cocoa then took a sip.

"That last number was the best."

"I thought so too." He took another drink. They sat, not looking at each other.

Libby tried to think of another safe topic, but it was too hard. She sipped her hot chocolate and waited for him to take a turn.

Nick drank his cocoa slowly, glancing around the parking lot occasionally. When students swarmed out of the restaurant toward the bus, shouting, teasing, and swatting at each other, the two of them watched in silence. A teacher spoke loudly but patiently to the youngsters, moving them onto the bus. At last the driver turned on the headlights, and the bus rolled out onto the street.

Nick sighed. "Were we that noisy?"

"I wasn't," Libby said.

"Me, either." He stuffed his plastic lid inside his empty cup. "Finished?"

"Yes."

He reached for her cup, and she handed it to him. Nick got

out, took the cups to a trash can, and returned to the truck.

"Really getting cold," he observed, starting the engine.

The hour-long ride down the highway was mostly quiet. Occasionally Libby made an effort, and twice Nick commented on the traffic without prompting, but each time, the words died away and the hum of the engine was the only sound.

Frustrated that she hadn't succeeded in drawing him out, engaging him in fascinating conversation, Libby felt inadequate. But after thirty miles she allowed herself to settle back against the seat and let her mind wander.

She had never been expert at talking to people she didn't know well. Parents' night was one thing, but men…

Her former fiancé, Aiden Knight, had always kept things rolling. He'd talked enough for both of them. Not boring, but outgoing. He was funny and interesting. She had liked him enormously, but always felt less than his match.

Aiden had insisted she captivated him, but she didn't know how. She could never think of clever replies to his remarks or keep up her side of a debate. She just let him have things his way. At first he said she was restful. At the end of their relationship, he changed that to reticent. He had met a woman who was more animated, more like himself, and it was over.

Tonight, she and Nick had heard some good music. The evening might have been better for them both, certainly easier, without the long ride each way, but it had been worthwhile. She could look back on it as a placid interlude. But she couldn't see it happening again. Nick had shown only minimal interest in her background and attitudes.

At last they were back in Waterville, and Nick drove to the church parking lot, where her Toyota sat, frozen and lonely.

As he parked the truck beside it, he said, "We ought to do this again."

She tried to say something but was too surprised to think of the appropriate response. A lump formed in her throat, making it impossible to talk.

"On purpose," Nick said.

He was peering at her. She nodded deferentially.

He opened his door and got out, reaching down between the seats for an ice scraper. "I'll get your windshield."

Zipping her jacket, she climbed down onto the pavement and reached for her purse. He was scraping the windshield of her car as she took her key ring from her pocket and unlocked the driver's door. She opened it and put her bag in on the front seat, then slid the key into the ignition. Nick had moved around to the passenger side and was flaking off the layer of frost.

"Not too bad yet," he said. "I'll just get the back window." He went to the rear of the car and made several passes with the scraper.

"Thanks," Libby said as he shook the frost off the blade.

"Better get in and get your engine warmed up," he said. "I'll wait 'til you get moving."

"All right. Thank you for taking me. For everything."

He nodded.

She got into the car and started it, turning the defroster on high, and sat for a minute waiting for the engine to warm. She looked over at his truck. Nick was inside but hadn't turned the headlights on. She put hers on and backed out carefully, and his lights came on.

The gray truck followed her out onto College Avenue, on out Elm Street and Silver Street, to Kennedy Drive. When she turned off on the road leading to the farmhouse, he tooted his horn and waved. She waved back, and he drove on. She felt suddenly chilly and nudged the switch from defrost over to heat.

Chapter 10

Learning to Shoot

Nick was up early Saturday, not willing to waste a minute of his day off. He'd planned to do some partridge hunting and gathered his gear quietly, eating breakfast alone in the kitchen. His thoughts kept straying back to the evening before and Libby Sharpe, quiet and uncommunicative. He'd wondered at first if she disliked him but had decided finally that she found it as hard to launch a discussion with a stranger as he did.

Maybe he'd botched it a little, telling her she didn't sound as though she loved her job, but it was the truth. He didn't see why people shouldn't enjoy their work.

Her large brown eyes had been luminous after the concert. She felt the music the way he did, and that had given him courage. But it was a long time since he had let a woman into his private life. Did he really want to do that?

His father, Justin Palmer, entered the kitchen just as Nick was rinsing out his cereal bowl.

"Where you off to?" His dad eyed the rifle and shotgun leaning in the corner near the door, and the knapsack beside it.

"Going to do some bird hunting. You want to go?"

"No, I guess not. I think I'll split a little wood."

"I'll help you with that later." Nick reached for his jacket. His parents were active and able to take care of themselves, but he tried to take as much of the heavy work from them as possible.

"Naw, that's my exercise," Justin said. "I sit at a desk all week now. Got to do something on the weekend."

Nick took a blaze orange vest from a peg beside the door and pulled it over his jacket.

"How was the concert?" his father asked.

"Good." Nick's mind snapped back to Libby.

"Who all went?"

"Oh, the new teacher."

"Miss Sharpe?"

"Yup." He zipped the vest and stooped to pick up the knapsack that held his ammunition.

"Who else?"

"Nobody."

Justin's eyes widened. "Just you and Miss Sharpe?"

"Yup." Nick felt slightly embarrassed as his father looked him up and down.

"Did you ride together?"

"Yup. My truck."

"I hope you were polite."

"Well, I tried my best, Dad. She doesn't talk much."

"And you do?"

Nick shrugged a little and picked up the two guns.

"You going out that way?" his dad asked suddenly.

"What way?"

"Tarlton Road."

"Why would I go out there?"

"You brought Mrs. Richardson's cookie tin home last week. Wouldn't hurt to return it." Justin walked over to the counter and picked up the tin.

Nick hesitated. "Sure, Dad."

***

Libby was about to call her mother for a second opinion on whether she ought to drive to Westbrook that morning when a knock sounded on the door.

"Just wanted to bring this back and say thank you for the cookies." Nick stood below her, at the bottom of the steps, with Kim's cookie tin in his hand. He passed it up to her, looking up for just a second, his brown eyes somber.

"Thanks. I'll tell Kim," Libby said. He was wearing jeans and a heavy blue jacket with an orange vest over it. His unexpected arrival left her tongue-tied, but she couldn't help wondering if he was disappointed to find that Kim wasn't home.

"Listen, do you have a hunting license?" he asked.

It seemed out of the blue, and it put Libby off balance. "No. I've never shot a gun in my life."

"Oh. I was going partridge hunting and I was thinking … maybe you'd want to go." Nick looked up at her, then away.

"Sorry." She wondered if she really was. She had been thinking she would go to Westbrook and come back that evening. But still, having Nick show up unexpectedly with an unconventional invitation was intriguing.

He hesitated. "Do you want to learn to shoot?"

She was surprised that he actually seemed to want to spend more time with her. That meant his suggestion last night had been more than courtesy. But guns. She smiled ruefully. "I'm not sure. I might hate it."

"That's okay. But you're not against hunting or anything, are you?"

"No. I grew up in town, and my dad wasn't into that. I just never had the opportunity."

"Look, I have today off. You want to try it? There's a gravel pit just down the road here. You know where I mean?"

She nodded.

"We could go over there and practice. I've got a .22 you can try. They're not real noisy. You might like it."

"Well …" The idea of going anywhere with him was appealing. He had an eager look, like Joey had when he came charging into the schoolroom with a butterfly cupped in his hands. But she had declared herself unready for a new

51

relationship, and she still believed that. She hadn't had time to properly put to rest her broken engagement.

"If you hate it, we'll quit," Nick said. "At least you'll know."

He seemed sincere, and Libby heard herself say, "All right."

"There you go. You should always be willing to try things, learn a new skill," he said, smiling broadly.

"What should I wear?"

He looked her over. "That's fine." She had on green corduroy pants and a cable knit sweater. "Better get a coat and hat. It's warming up, but it's still chilly."

She went for her things, dropping the cookie tin on the kitchen table and wondering what she was getting herself into. She climbed into the truck with him, and he drove a third of a mile down the road to where a dirt track led off between maple and birch trees, into an open gravel pit.

The bank on the far side was twenty feet high and irregularly gouged, where bucket loaders had scooped gravel into waiting dump trucks that summer. Nearer to them the sides of the pit were lower, with slopes running up to grassy areas that blended into brush, with trees rising beyond.

"The foliage is peaking early," Nick said, as they got out of the truck.

"Yes, I don't think it was as good as usual this year."

"Too dry last summer." He bent and picked up two empty beer cans, left behind by some weekend revelers, and walked toward the far side of the pit. He set them side by side on a large rock and came back toward her. She caught a faint whiff of wood smoke from the chimney of the nearest farmhouse.

From the truck, Nick brought a rifle and a box of cartridges. He showed her how to open the action and how the safety worked. Then he took some cartridges from the box, loaded the gun, and held it in a shooting position.

"Just hold it up against your right shoulder, like this." He held it out to her with the muzzle pointed skyward.

As she took the gun and swung it to her shoulder, the weight surprised her, and she found it hard to steady in front of her. She had a vague idea that she should point it at the cans.

"Let's go behind the truck, and you can rest it on the hood," Nick suggested.

He took the rifle and strode around the pickup, and Libby followed meekly. He demonstrated for her how she should stand. She had a vision of him putting his arms around her to steady the gun, like the hero in some old B movie, and had to suppress a giggle.

After handing her the rifle, he stepped aside. She leaned against the truck and rested her elbows on it, holding the barrel up with her left hand while her right grasped the stock.

"How's my form?"

He smiled. "Not bad. Now line up the sights."

"Huh?"

He touched a small piece of metal not far from her face. "Look through this groove." He ran his finger lightly along the barrel toward the end. "Line it up with this bead, so you can see it in the groove. Then point the bead at the bottom of one of the cans. It's simple."

It *was* simple. She was amazed.

"Now what?" she asked.

"Squeeze the trigger."

Chapter 11

Turn Around Slowly

Libby had to relinquish her position to look and see where her hand was in relation to the trigger. Nick watched her gravely without touching her or offering any more advice. When she had her right index finger gingerly poised on the trigger, she got back into the resting position and tried to remember everything.

"Take your time," he said. "Line up the sights."

She concentrated, first on the metal bead, then far beyond it to the tiny can twenty yards away. The barrel wavered.

"Take a deep breath and hold it," he said. "Then fire when you're ready."

She breathed deeply and adjusted, just a hair. Now or never. She squeezed. The report startled her, and she stood up. A puff of dust erupted from the bank behind the cans.

"Not bad," Nick said with a smile. "Try it again."

"Just shoot again?"

"Right, the gun loads itself for the next shot. You've got ten rounds in there. Try to just squeeze it gently. Don't jerk."

She got back into position. Sights, steady, squeeze. The dust puff was off to the left two feet.

"Easy. Just relax and take your time."

She went through it again. *Crack!* The dust swirl was just over the cans.

"That's better. You're going to hit it. Aim for the bottom

of the can."

On the ninth try, she hit it, and the can sprang into the air, then fell to the ground.

"Yes!" He slapped her on the shoulder. "All right!"

She laughed, looking at the fallen can, then at his gleaming eyes. He was thrilled, and she felt a little of his elation.

"Only took nine tries," she said sheepishly.

"That's not bad," he insisted. "You've got one more round."

She smiled and settled into position again, focusing on the second can. *Crack!*

"Oh, that was so close," Nick moaned. "I saw it wobble in the breeze when the bullet went by."

Libby shrugged. "Oh, well."

"If it was a deer it would have been close enough," he said. "Want me to reload for you?"

"Oh, I think I've had enough," she said. "Let me see you shoot."

"Nah."

"Yes. Come on. I want to see how it's done right."

He looked embarrassed, but he took a box of ammunition from his pocket and reloaded, smiling a little.

He didn't bother with resting on the hood of the truck. Libby stood back a pace as he swung the rifle up to his shoulder and put his eye close to the stock. It hung steady, just half a second, before he fired. The can jumped and fell to the ground.

She nodded slowly. "That's what I figured."

He met her eyes, and smiled a little, broader when she smiled back.

"Come on," he said.

They walked the length of the gravel pit, and he picked up another can along the way. He set the three on the rock and said, "Stand over here." Libby stepped to the spot he designated. He picked one can up in his left hand, hefted it, then tossed it high in the air. As it reached the peak of its flight, he swung the rifle up and fired. The can spun crazily as it fell.

Libby just stared at him, open-mouthed. He smiled, picked up another can and repeated the performance. When he had shot a hole in the third can, mid-air, he walked to where they had fallen and picked up two.

"Okay, this is the tricky part," he said.

"I can't wait." It was true. Her pulse was racing.

He tried throwing them both at once, but one fell inert to the ground as the other went high.

"Oops. Just a sec." He picked them up again and tossed them rapidly, first one, then the other, and whipped the rifle up, catching the first can when it was halfway down, then the second as it started to fall.

Libby clapped her hands gleefully. "I'm impressed!"

He shrugged and made a little bow.

"Tell me you practiced thousands of hours before you could do that."

"Six thousand, four hundred and seventeen," he said solemnly.

She laughed.

"So, you want to get a hunting license?"

"I'll consider it."

He nodded, evidently satisfied.

"You didn't mean today?" Libby faltered.

"Well, you'd have to take the hunter safety course before you could get a license."

"Oh. How does that work?"

"They usually give it on weekends. I know somebody who teaches it. If you want, I can check into it for you."

Her cheeks felt way warmer than they should. "I'm not sure. I mean—well, hunting. That's a major expedition. I don't have a gun. I don't even have one of those orange vests."

He laughed. "If you want to go, I can outfit you. My sister-in-law has everything. I'm sure she'd lend it to you, even her .22."

"You mean Jill?"

"Yeah. She likes to hunt. Shot a doe last November, up on Hampshire Hill."

"Really?" Libby couldn't picture Jill standing over a dead deer.

"Lots of venison in the freezer," Nick said. "Mike got an eight-point buck."

"How about you?"

"No, I didn't get one last year. I went out a couple of times, but I really didn't have time. We're pretty busy during hunting season."

"Where do you live?" Libby asked, suddenly curious. "Not with your brother?"

"No, I live with my folks."

"Oh." She hadn't figured that. It was endearing, somehow.

He caught her gaze. "What? You think that's weird?"

"No. I think it's nice. How old are they?"

"Not old. My dad's fifty-four. Mom's fifty-two."

She nodded. "They go to our church, don't they?"

"Yup."

"I lived with my parents until I came here."

"Yeah? You got any brothers and sisters at home?"

She shook her head. "I'm the youngest. My two brothers live down near Portland."

His eyebrows rose. He was interested, so she went on, "David works for a construction company. He's married and has three kids. Ben's a reporter. He's not married."

"For a newspaper?"

She smiled. "Yes. He's going to be the famous one of the family." Her hands were cold, and she shoved them into her jacket pockets.

He put his hand up suddenly, in a silencing motion. She froze and arched her brows.

"Turn around really slowly."

Chapter 12

Accident, Whim, or Necessity

Libby turned gradually until she faced the direction Nick did, toward the grassy berm of the gravel pit near the entrance.

"Fox," Nick whispered, near her ear.

She stood unmoving, searching the brush for a splash of orange.

"Under that big beech," Nick added.

Which tree was a beech? Not the majestically flaming red and orange sentinel. That had to be a maple. To the right of it, a smaller tree with smooth gray bark had a yellow flounce of outer leaves over its underskirt of green. Beneath its lowest branches was a dark, brownish form. It moved slightly.

"I see it," she breathed. They stood motionless.

The fox stared at them for several seconds, then it walked along the edge of the gravel pit and turned, scampering into the brush with the white tip of its tail bobbing.

"I'm surprised it came around with us shooting," Nick said. "But then, it's been a few minutes since we stopped firing. They're pretty shy."

"Wow. That was special."

"I hadn't seen one for a couple of months."

"I've never seen one before," Libby said.

"Really?"

"Really. It was smaller than I thought it would be. Like a cat. Well, bigger than a cat, but smaller than a dog."

"If you skinned it, it wouldn't be any bigger than a cat," Nick said. "Their fur fluffs up a lot. It must have a den up there somewhere close by."

"So that's a beech tree." Libby gazed thoughtfully at the tall, gray-barked tree.

"Yup. Want to see it up close?" They walked to the truck, and he unloaded the rifle and put it inside, then he mounted the gradual slope. Libby trekked along behind him, and soon was standing beneath the beech.

"Does it have nuts?" she asked.

"It might." He peered up into its heights. "I don't see any. Could be they fell and the squirrels got them all." He kicked at the leaves on the ground beneath the tree. "None here now, anyway. Some empty husks." He picked up a prickly brown pod, open and empty, and handed it to her.

"I'm ignorant," she said, scrutinizing it. "I never learned much about trees. I can tell a maple and a pine, and maybe an oak."

He smiled. "A beech will keep its leaves all winter."

"It will? But it's not an evergreen." Libby looked at the leaves.

"No, but the leaves just kind of fade to tan color, almost white, and hang on it till spring. When the new leaves start, they push the old ones off. If you see a tree in the woods in winter that has pale leaves, chances are pretty good it's a beech."

Libby reached out and tugged at a leaf. It didn't leave the branch easily. Though it was vibrant yellow, green still stained the end near the stem. She put it and the husk thoughtfully in her pocket. Looking up, she saw that Nick was watching her.

"To show my students." She laughed ruefully. "Although most of them probably already know more about beech trees than I do."

He smiled. "Some might, but not all of them. You ought to take them out to gather leaves. Make a scrapbook or something."

"That's a great idea. But I'll have to do some homework first."

"Come here." He stepped along the edge of the woods, where the trees were thicker.

"Know what tree this is?"

The yellow leaves were fat at the base and tapered at the end. The edge was jagged. She looked at the trunk and said, "Birch."

"Right. You know the bark. That one's easy. How about this one?" He took her to the base of a tall tree, six inches in diameter, with rough, furrowed dark gray bark at the bottom. Above her head, the bark became smooth and gray-green. The leaves were almost heart-shaped, with tiny teeth along the edges.

"I have no idea," Libby confessed.

"It's popple," he said. "That's what they call it around here. From the name poplar. It's really an aspen. It grows fast, but it's not good for much. The pulp mills take it, but it's not good for building or firewood."

"Poplar," said Libby. "I never would have known. Guess I'm not much of a teacher."

"Not everybody knows everything." He laughed. "Let me rephrase that. *Nobody* knows everything."

"How did you learn so much about trees?" she asked.

"Just tagging along after my dad in the woods. He taught me. But there's still a lot I don't know."

"A lot about trees? You're joking." Her eyes swept the near horizon, and she wondered how many species were within her view.

"Nope. Sometimes I have to look really hard before I can tell them, especially in winter. And once in a while I still find one I have to look up."

Her eyes went back to his face. He was peering at her intently.

"Look, you want to get some lunch?" he asked abruptly.

Her stomach lurched a little. In her mind, she saw Aiden,

smiling invitingly at her, the wind ruffling his hair as they stood before the library on the college campus.

"Have lunch with me," he'd coaxed. It was her senior year. She had given up on finding a husband at the college. She would go home to Maine and teach. If God had a husband for her, He would have to bring him to Maine. Aiden had appeared for the spring semester, a graduate assistant on loan from the secular university in the next town, to teach a class in statistics.

The time until graduation had been too short. She had gone home, but Aiden had written her, called her, e-mailed her. A year later, she had at last taken his pursuit seriously.

He came to Maine in August and drove along the coast with her. On a rocky beach at Reid State Park he had proposed, and she had accepted. But she was committed to teach another year at Gorham. He was teaching by then, at a private college in Kentucky. They had set the date for June twenty-fifth, the Saturday after her school year would end.

She was still sore from Aiden's precipitate rejection and breakup, and she didn't ever want to face that again. She looked deeply into Nick's eyes, searching for assurance, and wasn't sure she found it.

The shooting lesson and the nature walk had been fun, stimulating, but suddenly she was afraid of being disappointed again. She liked Nick a lot. If she let herself become attached to him and then he failed her, she didn't know if she could stand up to it. Better to back off now than to be cast off later.

"I—I really can't."

He didn't say anything.

Regret swept over Libby. He was feeling the rejection she was trying to avoid. Guilt would haunt her for inflicting that on him.

"If Kim were home," she said, stumbling to explain, "I'd ask you to eat lunch with us …"

His eyes cleared. "McDonald's?"

Irresolute, she glanced away, toward the pickup truck. "It wouldn't be a date, would it?"

Nick cocked his head, as if he was listening to the nuance in her question. "I think a date is something you make ahead of time." He smiled. "Either that, or it's something that grows on palm trees. I get confused."

She smiled. "I'm sorry. I guess I'm a little paranoid."

"You don't approve of dating?"

"It's not that." She turned toward him. "All right, I'll go, but I feel as though I ought to tell you, I'm not ready for dating. Not now." She shook her head. "I mean—well, that's it. I don't think I should date anyone right now."

He watched her face, weighing every word. "Well, we're not dating." He squinted a little with the effort of sorting out her declaration.

"Well, no. Last night wasn't a date. That was an accident."

"Right," Nick said, "and coming here today was … more of a whim."

She nodded soberly.

"And lunch," he said, "well, that would be … a necessity."

"A necessity?"

"Sure. We have to eat."

"Well, yes."

"Come on." They walked side by side down to the truck, and he opened the passenger door for her. Libby's stomach fluttered, and she grabbed the edge of the seat. He reached to help her in, but pulled his hand back before he touched her. When she was seated, he closed the door with a thoughtful expression and went around to the driver's side.

Chapter 13

Showing up at the Same Game

After Sunday school the next morning, Libby stood for a moment at the back of the church, her gaze running over the auditorium, evaluating the empty seats. Without Kim and Stacy, she could sit just about anywhere.

She felt most comfortable more than halfway back, and for the past five weeks she and the Richardsons had sat on the right side. Habit bred security. There was a half-empty pew three from the back, and she moved to it, sitting just in from the side aisle. When an elderly man and his wife came and took the empty spaces, she realized she had been hoping Nick would come and sit beside her.

He arrived after the offering and blended into the congregation on the other side of the church. She didn't see him look her way. Forcing her thoughts into order, she took out her notebook and prepared to outline the sermon, scolding herself for feeling disappointed. Adolescence was far behind her, and she ought not to be pining over a guy.

Irma Mitchell, the twins' mother, engaged her in conversation in the side aisle when the service was over, and Libby thought Nick would be gone, his stolen lunch hour expired, by the time she got outside. She shook hands with Pastor Wilson and emerged into cool sunlight, her eyes going quickly to the railing where Nick had waited the week before. Two high school girls lounged there, laughing together over a shared secret.

She walked slowly around the corner toward her car. Nick was leaning against it on the driver's side, his arm resting on the roof, his crisp green uniform giving him an air of assurance and competence. Her spirits lifted and she smiled, walking quickly toward him.

"Hello."

"Hi." A hint of a smile tugged at the corners of his mouth. "I got held up this morning with a call, but that means I have twenty minutes left for lunch."

"Are all wardens as strict as you about their lunch hours?"

"I doubt it. But I don't want to short the state."

"Of course not."

"I brought you this." He held out a soft-covered book.

"*Trees of the Eastern United States.* Thank you! I was going to try to get to the library tomorrow." Libby thumbed through it. "This is great. I'll return it in a couple of weeks."

"No, you can keep it. It's for you."

She blushed, embarrassed at the pleasure his gesture brought. She tucked the book on top of her Bible. "Thanks very much."

"I've been thinking about yesterday." Nick nodded gravely at Drew Griffin, the youth minister, who walked past them with his wife and called a greeting. A three-year-old boy hung on to Diane Griffin's hand.

Libby cast a worried glance after the Griffins. Drew's smile was a little too smug. She wondered how well he knew Nick, and what conclusions he drew from seeing them standing together next to Libby's car.

"What about yesterday?" she asked.

"It was fun."

"What, shooting cans?"

He shrugged. "Everything. The cans, the fox, the trees … lunch. Our second non-date."

Her eyes snapped up to his. He was teasing, but not maliciously, she decided.

66

"There's a concert Friday at Colby College," he said. "Brass ensemble. Will you come to it?"

She was shaking her head before he finished. "I don't think so."

"Come on, you love good music."

She looked back toward the front of the church, where the stream of people from the door was slackening. "Thank you, Nick. It sounds great, but … that would be …"

"A date?" He craned his neck, trying to see her whole expression. "Because I would beg to differ on that. It wouldn't be. Not really. See, it's like this. My dad really loves baseball. Now, if I'm going to a Red Sox game, and I tell my dad about it and he decides to go too, that's not a date. It's just two people who like baseball showing up at the same game. Not a date. Really." His eyes were serious, ingenuous.

She smiled and closed her eyes, shaking her head. "That's not what I was going to say."

"Oh, it's not?" he asked dubiously. The smile was gone, and his eyes were meltingly focused on hers.

"I was going to say that would be the night Kim asked me to babysit so she can go to a meeting."

"I see." He turned his uniform hat slowly in his hands. "So, you wouldn't be opposed to going to a concert sometime, the same night I was going, if you didn't have a previous commitment?"

"Can I think about it?"

"I wish you would."

"Hey, Nick!" They both turned toward the hearty voice. Mike Palmer and his family were opening their car doors across the aisle. The teal minivan was one of the few vehicles left in the lot.

"Hey," Nick yelled. To Libby, he said apologetically, "My brother."

She nodded.

Joey detached himself from the family and ran to them.

"Uncle Nick, are you coming over today?"

"Boy, I don't know, Joey, I'm on duty today, and—" he glanced at his watch. "My lunch hour is over in fifteen minutes. How about if I come for supper?"

Mike had approached behind his son. "Tonight?" he asked. "Sure. I'll call Mom and tell her not to expect you. Be there at five."

"If I can," Nick said.

"Well, the kids have to be here early for their clubs tonight."

"Okay, I'll try."

Mike hesitated, glancing at Libby. "If you'd like to bring someone …"

Nick said, "Oh, I don't think so. I'll be coming right from work. Thanks."

Mike nodded. "Okay, we'll look for you as close to five as you can make it." He nodded at Libby. "Miss Sharpe."

"Libby," she said.

"Libby?"

"Well, it's Elizabeth. My mother's maiden name was Libby, so they called me that." Her face warmed with the annoying blush that had plagued her lately.

"Well, nice to see you." Mike took Joey back to the van.

Nick watched silently as the family settled into the vehicle and Mike drove away. He turned back to Libby.

"Elizabeth?" he asked.

"Yes."

"Huh. So, I didn't mean to be rude about what Mike said. Would you have gone if I'd asked you?"

"I—don't—"

He nodded. "That's what I thought."

She stared down at the tips of her black flats, embarrassed. "I'm sorry. I think I'm the one who's been rude."

He shook his head. "It would have been a date."

Cautiously, she looked up from under her eyelashes to see if he was laughing. He wasn't. "Your logic was flawless," she said.

"About the baseball game?"

"Yes. If that were to happen … it would be quite a coincidence if you and your father … had seats together. I mean, Fenway Park …"

He looked past her shoulder, toward the parsonage and the river beyond, shaking his head. "No such thing. As a coincidence, I mean."

Feeling quite daring, she said slowly, "If you find there's another night when you're free and there's another concert … or a baseball game, or maybe a play or a lecture on trees …"

"You would go?" he asked.

"I might."

He nodded gravely. "I'll keep it in mind. Elizabeth." He put on his hat and walked away.

Chapter 14

A Proposal

Kim and Stacy arrived, tired out from the long drive, at four thirty that afternoon. Stacy wore a new purple sweatshirt with Winnie the Pooh on the front. Her face and hands were sticky, and she smelled fruity. Libby picked her up in a huge hug.

"I'm so glad you're home, Stacy. You were gone a long time!"

Kim embraced her, too. "You survived the weekend without us. Did you go home yesterday?" She unlocked the trunk of the black Saturn.

"No." Libby reached for a suitcase. "Actually, I had a very surprising weekend."

"Surprising?" Kim's eyebrows rose.

"We love surprises," said Stacy.

Kim handed the little girl a pillow and set their bags out onto the driveway. She and Libby managed to haul them all inside in one trip.

"What smells so good?" asked Kim.

"Meatloaf and baked potatoes, in the oven."

"You've gone to a lot of trouble."

"No, no trouble." Libby set down the luggage she carried. "I enjoyed it. Are you hungry now?"

"Famished. Stacy's probably not, though. She's been eating crackers and gummy fruit all the way up here." Kim turned to her daughter and said, "Go wash up."

Libby began to set the table, putting Kim's iris-decorated china plates out for the three of them.

"So, tell me all," Kim said darkly. "Quick, before Stacy comes back."

Libby smiled.

"Well, I went to the concert in Bangor Friday night."

"Did you? Good. Did you enjoy it?"

"Yes, it was very uplifting." She laid the silverware out carefully.

"And?"

Libby smiled and set a spoon at Stacy's place. "I learned to shoot a rifle Saturday."

"What? What are you saying? Tell me!"

Libby smiled cryptically.

Kim's eye fell on the green cookie tin with a Currier and Ives scene on the lid. "Oh! Someone's been here. The cookie tin is back." She eyed Libby speculatively. "Did you and Nick Palmer have a date?"

"No, we most definitely did not have a date." Libby pushed her dark hair back behind her ears and picked up two potholders off the counter. "Could you get me a trivet, please?"

Stacy came running back from the bathroom, and the three soon sat down to the meal.

Spearing a tomato slice from her salad, Kim said thoughtfully, "Okay, I would say that Nick has to be the one who showed you how to shoot. Right or wrong?"

"Right. He was also the one who drove me to the concert."

"Ooh. The plot thickens."

Libby laughed and told her roommate the story of the embarrassing encounter of the concert-goers in the church parking lot and the laconic drive to Bangor and back.

"I don't know Nick very well, but I think he's the quiet type," Kim said. "Game wardens have to be, don't they?"

"I don't know about that. But by the time we got back that night, I'd decided he really hated me and could hardly wait to drop me off and get out of there. Then he said we ought to do it again sometime."

Kim laughed delightedly. "That's priceless. You will tell your grandchildren about that night."

"And then there was yesterday," Libby said diffidently.

"Yes, the shooting match."

"It wasn't a shooting match. He took me to the gravel pit, and we shot a few cans. It was fun. I couldn't believe it. I actually had fun shooting beer cans."

"Did the two of you exchange more than ten words the whole time?"

"Yes, we did."

"Fantastic." Kim's eyes gleamed. "Do you like him, Libby? Of course you do, or you wouldn't have gone out with him."

"Is that what I did?" Libby asked. "Because I was really trying to keep it out of the dating mode. Nick and I agreed it wasn't a date."

"Mommy, I need butter," Stacy said.

Kim pulled over the butter dish and spread some on Stacy's potato. "Why?" she asked. "You don't want to date him? It sounds like a pretty agreeable thing to me."

Libby hesitated. "I don't know as I want to be dating anyone right now."

"Because of what happened in your last relationship?"

"I guess so." She considered that and faced Kim. "I feel like I must have missed something, misread some signals somewhere with Aiden. Our courtship was mostly long distance, but he seemed so sincere. I think he was sincere, but … something happened."

"Absence does *not* usually make the heart grow fonder." Kim helped Stacy with the salad dressing.

"Not?" Libby asked.

"Well, you were how far away? A thousand miles?"

"Something like that," Libby agreed miserably.

"And you set the date for how far in the future?"

"Ten months."

"That's a long time."

"Some people have long engagements," Libby said defensively. "I had a contract with the school district."

"I'm not saying it was wrong. I'm just saying it was a long time." Kim's voice was gentle. "And then, he met someone close at hand. Someone he could see anytime. Is that the way it was?"

"I guess so." Libby laid down her fork. She'd lost her appetite.

"Aunt Libby, don't be sad," Stacy said. "Mr. Palmer got the bad guys."

Libby and Kim smiled.

Brushing her daughter's hair off her forehead, Kim said, "She's so tired. I really ought to put her to bed and stay home tonight, but I want to go to church."

"I can stay with her."

"No, let's just put her in her fuzzy p.j.s and let her sleep on the pew," Kim said. "If we hurry, we can get the back row and no one will notice."

In the car on the way to church, Libby asked, "Do you ever think you'll get married again?" It was nearly dark, and she couldn't see Kim's profile distinctly.

Kim said slowly, "Sometimes I think it would be good. For me and for Stacy. That is, if it was the right man." She glanced at Libby and said, "Don't panic, but I had a proposal yesterday."

Libby stared at her.

Kim nodded. "It was a man in my home church. His wife died of cancer three or four years ago. He's a lot older than me, nearly forty. But ... he'd heard at church that I was going to be home visiting my folks, and he called and asked if he could see me. He said he knew it was sudden, but he'd been praying about it. He felt God wanted him to ask me to marry him."

"That is bizarre," Libby cried. "What did you say?"

"I said I was flattered, and I would consider it carefully."

"Really?"

"Well, I figured I had to. He wasn't whacko. It's not like he's hearing voices. He'd been praying a lot lately about the possibility of finding a wife. He thought it was providential that I was coming home now."

Libby shook her head. "How long are you going to consider it?"

"Until I know whether or not I should accept, or he takes the offer off the table."

"Do you know him at all? Is he a nice man?"

"Oh, yes, I wouldn't consider it if he weren't. Eric and I knew them. We visited in their home before Mrs. Franklin died. He's very intelligent. He's a psychologist."

"A Christian psychologist?"

"Yes. He has two children, a girl sixteen, and a boy thirteen."

"And you are seriously considering this?"

Kim hesitated. "I am. But I'll tell you, right now I'm leaning toward saying no. Will you pray about it? My feeling is that if this is of God, He's got to clue me in on it. I can't just accept what some man tells me as being the truth. I'm praying hard about it and looking for guidance in Scripture."

"Does Stacy like him?"

"She only saw him once. Hard to say."

Chapter 15

You Knocked Him Out

Still wearing his uniform, Nick was waiting in the church parking lot beside his truck when Kim drove in. He walked toward the car with more confidence than he'd felt since the night the poachers were caught.

"Hello, Mrs. Richardson. Did you have a nice trip?"

"Yes, thank you, Nick, and please call me Kim."

He nodded. He smiled as Libby got out, pretty and flushed, her hair up on her head in a knot that looked simple but solid. He peered through the back door's window at Stacy.

"Looks like the little one's asleep," he said. "May I carry her for you?"

"Thank you," Kim said. "She's exhausted. I was hoping we'd get here in time to sit in the back."

Nick opened the door and unbuckled Stacy, carefully hoisting her in his arms until her head rested on his shoulder. He was used to carrying his brother's babies. It always brought him a tenderness, to hold someone so vulnerable and trusting.

They walked briskly into the church. The parking lot was filling, and parishioners were moving into the sanctuary. The back row on the right was already occupied, and Nick moved with authority into the last row on the left side of the church, laying Stacy gently on the pew pad. Kim went around the far end of the row and came in on the other side, sitting down at her daughter's head and thanking Nick.

He settled onto the pew and smiled at Libby as she sat down beside him, smoothing the skirt of her blue dress.

"Did you have a nice time at your brother's?" she asked.

"Well, I got the third degree," he said apologetically.

"What for?"

"You." He watched her reaction.

"I was afraid of that. This morning, people were staring in the parking lot." Libby glanced around fretfully. "I suppose it will be even worse tonight. Are you sure you want to sit here?"

"Yes." He'd never been surer of anything in his life, but he didn't want to embarrass her.

"They might—" she stopped abruptly.

He looked at her levelly. "Would that be so terrible?"

Libby's eyes were troubled. "People make assumptions."

He wanted to ease her nervousness, but the pastor stood up then, ending the conversation, and Libby faced the front. Nick determined that sometime later he would find a way to persuade her that what other people thought didn't matter.

***

Libby slowly brought her mind onto the service. She was getting a new perspective, sitting on the left side of the church, and sitting beside Nick Palmer.

She could see the stained glass window on the right front side of the auditorium. She couldn't see it when she sat near the back of the other side. It portrayed a storm-tossed boat on violent blue and purple water, with Christ walking steadily across the surface. Usually she saw the window across from it, the one with Jesus holding a baby on his lap and toddlers crowding about his knees.

Libby made her breathing steady and rhythmic. The exercise was wasted when the pastor called the first hymn and Nick held out the hymnbook for her to share. Her pulse rioted.

It was ludicrous. She was beyond this. Wasn't she? Perhaps Aiden had set her back so far that she had to go through the awkward, emotion-tearing phase again. She began to pray silently, but she wasn't sure for what.

When the service ended, Nick carried Stacy to the car and said good night cordially to Kim and Libby.

"Could I call you?" he asked Libby in a low voice, the car door between them as she prepared to enter Kim's Saturn.

"Yes, I guess so." She swallowed hard. Nick was determined to make progress, and she wasn't so sure anymore that she was against that.

He pulled out his cell phone and tapped it. She whispered the number, and he entered it. Then he looked up and smiled. "Thanks. I promise not to be a pest."

***

Libby had worked hard on Saturday evening and Sunday afternoon, planning to integrate the topic of trees into her classroom lessons. The class would gather and display leaves, needles, cones and nuts.

She had found an oak tree on the edge of the hayfield behind the house and gathered a coffee can full of acorns that the children could use as math counters and for art projects. She had located several new poems, and a story about a pioneer family gathering beechnuts and butternuts in the woods.

The children were excited on Monday, full of energy and weekend stories. She got permission to take them outside but saved the leaf gathering for the last period of the afternoon. Each child received a plastic bag to hold his treasures.

They found pine, spruce, fir, maple, apple, oak, willow, birch, ash, and a tree Libby couldn't identify. It had long brown pods hanging from it in clusters. They picked several pods and a handful of leaves, and she looked carefully at the bark. She would look it up later, when she could sit down with the tree book.

No phone call came that evening. Libby found the mystery tree in the guide—a black locust. She went to bed at nine thirty, scolding herself once again for feeling let down. He hadn't said when he would call.

Tuesday she allocated a large block of time for the children to mount their leaves and prepare their exhibits.

Joey Palmer came to her desk shyly and said, "Miss Sharpe, my Uncle Nick thinks you're pretty."

Libby blushed. "That's very flattering, Joey."

"I think so, too." His huge brown eyes beamed at her.

"Thank you." She hoped none of the other children had heard him, knowing her face was scarlet.

"And my mom says you're smart and you can borrow her rifle."

Libby laughed. "Joey, I'm not sure you should be telling me what other people say about me."

"How come? My dad said you knocked him out."

"What?" She tried to make sense of that.

"No, that's not right. You got knocked out."

"I don't think that's quite what he said, Joey."

"Yes, when Uncle Nick came, Daddy said, 'That Miss Sharpe is knocked out.' And Uncle Nick said, 'You're telling me.' "

Libby said doubtfully, "I think you must have heard him incorrectly."

"Well, you said your name is Lizbeth. Is that right?"

"Yes, it's Elizabeth. But you must call me Miss Sharpe."

"I will." He smiled adoringly. "But Uncle Nick calls you Lizbeth."

***

On Tuesday evening, Libby and Kim paid household bills together. The electric bill and the rent were divided, and Libby wrote Kim a check for her share.

"The oil truck is supposed to come this week," Kim said. "I'm not sure how much is in the tank, but we're using it every night now. I hope they come soon."

"Mm." Libby looked up at her, lost in thought. "I'm thinking of using a twins theme for November. What do you think?"

"Because of April and Ashley?"

"Yes, they got me thinking about it. It might be fun for the kids, learning how twins are alike and different at the same time. Or do you think April and Ashley get too much attention already?"

"I don't know. They certainly thrive on it." Kim put away her checkbook and stacked up the paid bills and the envelopes to be mailed.

"Last year I did a Thanksgiving theme, but it seemed to go on too long. Maybe a week of that is enough," Libby mused. "We could do twins the first couple of weeks, then do the Pilgrims and Thanksgiving for a week and a half before vacation."

"Sounds like a lot of work for you," Kim said.

"Well, I have all the Thanksgiving things planned already from last year. I can just pick the very best activities from my file. The twins thing would take some work. But it would be really different and interesting, don't you think?"

"Sure. Ask Irma Mitchell to help you prepare. She might have some articles and insights."

"Great idea."

"I'm glad I don't have to do bulletin boards and art projects," Kim said. "We barely get through the academics."

Kim's phone rang. Libby sat still as she answered it.

"Hello? Oh, hi, Madeline. No, I hadn't thought about it yet."

Libby gathered her papers from the table and went upstairs to her bedroom to go through her file boxes for teaching aids. She was being such an idiot, caring that Nick hadn't called. She shouldn't have let her hopes rise so high.

She stared at herself in the mirror over her dresser. What had she expected? She had told him she didn't want to date, had pushed him away every time he made overtures.

Her brown eyes were wary, distrustful. What man would want to meet that viewpoint head-on? She pulled the covered elastic from the bottom of her braid and brushed her hair out. Nick had enough of a struggle mustering his own self-assurance, let alone troubling about hers. But still, he had asked if he could call.

Chapter 16

Something Worth Keeping

Libby worked hard at school on Wednesday, and the children were especially active. After classes ended she had the duty of seeing the students safely onto their buses or into their parents' cars. When they were gone, she went back to her classroom and spent an hour working on decorations and lesson plans.

Kim had gone home before her, taking Stacy, and had supper ready when Libby dragged in at five o'clock.

"You should stay home tonight," Kim told her. "You have black circles under your eyes. You're working too hard."

Libby shook her head. "I didn't sleep very well last night. And Marty Begin was in top form today. I had to speak to him about thirty times. I think that boy is my biggest challenge."

"Give him a special job to do tomorrow," Kim suggested. "He wants your attention."

Libby sighed. "I let him hold the tacks for me today when I was hanging up the spelling papers. He dropped the box, and they went all over the floor. By some miracle, nobody stepped on one, but it took us ten minutes to pick them up and get everyone settled down again."

"I've had days like that."

Libby roused herself to consider her friend's needs. "I've been praying for you and your future. Any developments?"

"Not yet." Kim smiled regretfully. "I don't think it's going to happen.

"No?"

"I just don't feel marriage is right for me at this time."

"Are you going to tell him?"

Kim nodded. "He said he'll call me Friday night, or I could call him anytime before that if I had an answer. I don't think I'm ready to call him yet, but … If nothing changes before Friday evening, I'll tell him to look elsewhere."

"It might be good for you and Stacy," Libby suggested.

"I know. It would be in some ways, I'm sure. To be taken care of again." She sighed. "But love is important, Libby. Don't you think so?"

"It is. But you might love him if you knew him better."

"Yes, I might. But I can't tell from here. And I don't think I want one of those long-distance courtships, like you had."

That stung, and Libby kept quiet. If she'd spent more time with Aiden and known him better, would she still have wanted to marry him?

***

There was no sign of Nick at the church that night, and Libby sat silently fighting sleep through the hymn, the Bible lesson, and the prayer requests. It was nearly seven thirty when he came quietly in through the double door and dropped onto the pew beside her. His uniform was wrinkled, and he smelled of cigarette smoke. Libby turned to smile at him, but her nose crinkled.

"Smoky?" he whispered.

She nodded.

"Sorry. Ray's car." He was quiet until it was time to break up for prayer groups. "We've been working every night," he said then, apologetically. "I'm out with Tom or Ray half the night. I've got to go right out again when church is over. I'm sorry. I meant to call you." He looked anxiously after the men who were leaving the auditorium for prayer in other rooms, then back at Libby.

"It's okay," she said.

"Well, if I don't see you again tonight, I'll be sorry, but it doesn't mean—"

"You can't help it," she said.

He nodded with relief and walked quickly toward the doorway to the classroom area. Libby found she was smiling. He hadn't forgotten, and he wanted to be sure she knew that.

When the prayer groups came back and the pastor stood before them to close the service, Nick stopped briefly at the corner of the pew, looking at the clock over the back door. "I've got to run," he whispered.

Libby nodded and smiled, and he was gone.

***

On Thursday evening, Libby received a phone call from Jill Palmer.

"Miss Sharpe, I was wondering if you would join our family for dinner tomorrow evening?"

"I'm sorry, but I'm babysitting for my roommate tomorrow night. Thank you for the invitation, Mrs. Palmer."

"Oh, well, please call me Jill. Nick told me you were babysitting, and I thought perhaps you could bring Stacy with you. If Mrs. Richardson doesn't mind, that is. Nick especially requested that I invite you both."

"Nick did?" Libby felt the nerves returning, full force.

"Yes. He'll be here, and he asked me to invite you. I was very happy to do it. Won't you come?"

"Well, I—I'm not sure. I'll have to ask Kim."

"Of course. Oh, and Nick impressed upon me that this is not a date, if that makes any difference. It's just a chance to get acquainted with the family of one of your students."

There was a long pause as Libby tried to frame a reply that wouldn't sound idiotic. She wondered just how funny Jill Palmer thought this struggling relationship was.

"Miss Sharpe?"

"Yes," she said. "Please call me Libby. I'll—ask Kim. Could I call you back, please?"

Kim was enthusiastic about the plan. "His family wants to get better acquainted with you. That is so proper and sweet! And Mike and Jill Palmer are a great couple. Of course you can take Stacy. Will his parents be there?"

"I hope not," Libby said. "That would be way too much. Do you really think I should go?"

"Yes! Libby, this is *good*."

"I—" she shrugged futilely.

"Still think you're not ready to date?" Kim asked.

"This isn't a date."

"Of course it is. Nick set it up in advance. It's a date."

"Then I don't want to do it."

"Oh, Libby, it's only a word. Call it something else if it will make you feel better. The man wants to spend time with you, and he wants his family to get to know you."

Libby said a bit plaintively, "I wish I knew how he really feels about this, and what he said to Jill."

Kim sat down in a chair, face to face with Libby. Her blonde ponytail hung over her shoulder as she leaned forward. "Are you embarrassed that he wants to see you?"

"No. I guess I'm embarrassed that I want to see him, after I told him I don't want to date. I meant it when I said it, but he's worked his way around that barrier somehow."

Kim asked softly, "Do you still think about your ex-fiancé?"

"Aiden?"

"Yes, that guy."

"Sometimes. I can't help it."

"Do you still love him?"

"I don't know. Sometimes I think I never really knew him well enough. He hurt me terribly, but I think … it must be best this way. I mean, would you want to live the rest of your life with a man who would break an engagement at the last minute like that? Or a man who didn't but wished he had?"

"No, I wouldn't," said Kim. "Do you really believe God wants you with Aiden?"

"I guess not, or I'd be married to him now," Libby said.

"And do you think God wants you to stay single forever?"

"I hope not. But still, that doesn't mean I should jump at the first man who comes along, does it?"

Kim sighed. "Is that the way you see Nick?"

"Well, he *is* the first man who came along. If I do get close to another man, I want to go slowly and really get to know him."

"You knew Aiden for more than two years, didn't you?"

"Yes, but we didn't have a chance to spend much time together. I think that's what tore us apart, really."

"Then spend time with Nick. Talk to him about all the things that concern you. Get to know his mind, his attitudes, his peeves. And if you come up against something that doesn't feel right, back off."

Libby looked down at the braided rug that covered the middle of the living room floor. Kim's mother had sewed it years before, cutting strips from old wool skirts. The blues and browns and reds blended softly into harmonious warmth. If she could take the shreds that were left of her feelings and piece them together like that somehow, she might have something worth keeping.

Libby picked up her phone and tapped on the recent calls and Jill's number. "Mrs. Palmer? It's Libby."

"Yes, and it's Jill."

"Stacy and I will come."

Chapter 17

Like Jumping a Deer

Libby dressed carefully Friday evening in a new calf-length olive skirt, beige blouse and tapestry vest.

"You two just have a great time," Kim said as she zipped Stacy into her winter jacket over brown corduroy overalls. "If you're not here when I get home, I'll just figure you're in good company."

"What if Mr. Franklin calls while you're gone?" Libby asked.

"He'll call back," Kim said. "My meeting probably won't last more than a couple hours." The high school and junior high staff and parents planned to discuss proposed changes in the sports and extra-curricular programs.

She waved to them as Libby drove out and headed toward town, following her phone's GPS for directions.

The Palmers' home was a modest ranch house in a quiet residential neighborhood on the fringe of Waterville. Libby knew Mike was manager of the Agway store, across the river in Winslow. The open garage door revealed the minivan the family drove to church, and a ten-year-old pickup truck was parked in the driveway, next to Nick's state vehicle.

Libby unbuckled Stacy and walked with her uncertainly toward the house. Nick came out through the garage door, smiling.

"Come in this way." He was in his uniform, but looked

less harried than he had Wednesday night. He guided them past the van, through the laundry room, and into the kitchen, where Jill was mashing potatoes in a large kettle.

"Hi, Libby, we're so glad you could come. Hello, Stacy." Jill's light hair was held back by a large barrette. She had a long chef's apron over jeans and a green knit shirt. Libby felt she was overdressed in her skirt and blouse.

Rachel Palmer came in from the next room crying, "Stacy, Stacy! Come see my toy horses."

Libby helped Stacy remove her coat and let Rachel lead her away. "She's in kindergarten, right?" Jill asked.

"Yes."

"Rachel's in first grade. They see each other a lot at school, I guess."

"You want to sit down?" Nick asked as he took Libby's coat and Stacy's.

"Well, maybe I could help Jill," Libby said tentatively.

"We're almost ready to eat," Jill said. "Just go ahead in and say hi to Mike, and I'll yell in a minute."

Nick took her through the dining area to the living room, dropping the jackets on a chair. Mike stood up from his recliner with a stack of math flashcards in his hand. Joey sat on the floor at his feet.

"Libby, glad to see you." Mike extended his right hand, and she shook it.

"I see you and Joey are brushing up your multiplication tables," she said.

"Yes, we took you seriously. It's our nightly routine. Flashcards first, then we play a game."

"That's great," Libby said. "I've seen some improvement in Joey's math. He's getting quicker on his speed drills."

Mike smiled as she and Nick sat down on the couch. Libby looked around. The furniture was modest and showed some wear. A large bookcase stood against one wall, holding an encyclopedia, some reference books, novels, and a row of children's books.

"I like to see lots of books in a home," she said to Mike.

"Oh, that's not half of it," he said. "I haven't had much time to read lately, but Jill is a bookworm. Joey's turning into one, too." He reached down and ruffled his son's hair. Joey was carefully fitting the flashcards into their box.

A squeal came from the next room, and Mike called, "Rachel! What's Amy doing?"

"She's okay, Daddy. She's playing with Stacy and me."

Jill came to the dining room doorway in her apron and said, "Guess it's ready. Can you get the kids?"

Mike went toward the room where the girls were playing and herded the three little ones toward the kitchen. Joey, Nick and Libby followed.

Jill directed everyone to their seats, putting Libby between Nick and Stacy. Rachel sat on Stacy's other side, proprietary of her visitor. Beyond Nick, Mike sat at the head of the table.

Joey scowled. "I want to sit by Uncle Nick."

"Joey," said Mike sternly.

The boy frowned and sat down between Rachel and Jill, and Mike asked the blessing for their meal of baked chicken, potatoes, squash, green beans, and biscuits.

"Do you have a garden?" Libby asked.

"Yes, it's about done this year," Jill said. "There are a few carrots and beets out there yet that I've got to get in."

Libby learned that the vegetables on the table were all from the Palmers' garden. She thought she and Kim might have a small garden the next summer, since Kim seemed to have decided to stay in the farmhouse. She wondered if Mr. Franklin had called yet and gotten the bad news.

Nick ate quietly, and his brother pumped Libby for information on her family and her attitude toward her new community.

"I like it here," Libby said. "It's a lot different from where I grew up. More rural. The children seem more relaxed, not so hurried somehow."

"Now, that's a good description of Nicholas," said Jill.

"Laid back."

Libby glanced at Nick, who placidly went on eating. Tonight he was much calmer than the nervous, fretful man he'd been on the night they had driven to Bangor together.

"Easy going Nick," Mike agreed.

Libby was beginning to wonder if she had seen only Nick's worst side. But she thought of the way he'd shot the cans out of the air and decided you couldn't do that if you were tense.

When the meal was over, Libby insisted on helping Jill with the dishes. Nick looked the slightest bit wistful as Mike took him out into the garage to look under the hood of Jill's van.

***

"She's a peach," Mike said, opening his toolbox and selecting a wrench.

Nick peer at the engine and started unscrewing the wing nut on top of the air cleaner.

"You think this is going somewhere?" Mike probed.

"Jill's van?"

Mike laughed. "Right."

Nick wasn't ready to discuss Libby with his brother, although he was glad Mike and Jill had consented to host them for dinner.

"She and Jill will get along," Mike said.

Nick nodded. Outgoing Jill was perfect for Mike, and he thought she would draw Libby out too. "I hope they can be friends."

Mike lifted the air cleaner, and Nick shone the drop light on the carburetor. "You need to rebuild this thing."

"Think so?"

"Yup. You don't want Jill to get stranded somewhere."

"Listen, Nicky, anytime you need someplace to take a girl, you can bring her here, if you want to. I mean, you know,

92

games or videos, whatever. Kind of a low-key thing."

Nick nodded. Libby was definitely low-key, and he thought the family atmosphere would reassure her. He glanced at Mike. "I tried to get her to go to a concert with me at Colby tonight, but she wouldn't."

"Well, go slow. It's like jumping a deer, you know? If you come up on them too fast, they take off and you never catch up."

"Jill's not like that." It was a simple statement of fact.

"You're right. Jill stood still and just kind of let me walk up to her. Some women can do that. Libby seems like she's scared of something."

Nick was surprised Mike was so intuitive. He might have expected the repeated retreat from a younger girl. Libby had definitely been burned somewhere along the way.

"Well, I just want to make sure she's never scared of *me*," he said.

"Then do what you're doing."

Chapter 18

Rock Solid

"Nick says you might go hunting sometime?" Jill asked, running dishwater into the sink. There was no dishwasher.

"I don't know," Libby said. "He mentioned it once, but we didn't make it definite."

"Well, if you need anything, just holler. I've got hunting gear and a .22 and a deer rifle. Nick might have an extra deer gun. I'm not sure what he's got right now. Mike bought me one a couple of years ago, a .308. He *said* it was for me, but I think it was really for him." She laughed.

"Do you like to hunt?" Libby asked. "I've never been before."

"It's fun with the guys. I'm not real fond of sitting for hours in the woods if it's freezing cold. But I got a doe last fall—my first deer. It was exciting. Mike did the field dressing. I wouldn't like that part." Jill washed the dinner plates and stacked them in a drainer, and Libby wiped them carefully, one by one.

"I don't have a license or anything," she said.

Jill nodded. "You'd have to take the hunter safety course if you've never had one. It may be too late for this year."

Libby felt a little relief. "I don't know as I'd have time right now. If they offer it in the summer, maybe I could take it for next year."

"That would be a good idea, if you intend to hang around

with Nick much." Jill glanced at Libby then stopped, her hands in the dishwater. "I'm sorry. I forgot, this isn't a—" She smiled a little, self-reproaching. "Nick will kill me."

Libby picked up another plate and said carefully, "What exactly did he say, if I may ask?"

Jill gritted her teeth and swung around to look toward the laundry room, where the garage door was just visible.

"I'm not sure I should tell you." She smiled and wrung out the dish cloth, then began wiping the counter. "I like you, Libby."

"Thanks. I like you, too." Libby waited, the dish towel hanging from her hand.

Jill tossed the cloth into the sink and began pulling containers for the leftovers from a cabinet. "All I know is, he was adamant that this is not a date for you two. Do you know anything about that?"

Libby felt her face reddening. "I guess I do."

"So, you and Nick aren't dating?"

"No. We're not."

"Well, that's what he said. This is not a date, it's just a family thing."

Libby sighed. "Maybe I'm kidding myself."

Jill scraped squash into a round plastic container and looked at Libby. "Well, you're not kidding Nick. He wants to date you."

Libby took a handful of silverware from the dish drainer and began drying it thoughtfully. Jill opened a drawer with a plastic silverware tray inside, for her to place it in.

"If you don't want to talk about this, it's okay." Jill smiled and began washing the serving dishes.

"How long have you known Nick?" Libby asked.

"A long time. Mike and I have been married eleven years. I guess I knew him three or four years before that."

They worked in silence for a minute, and Jill began putting away the dishes Libby had dried.

"Has he had girlfriends?" Libby asked at last.

Jill shook her head. "Not many. The last one I would call a girlfriend was ages ago. We're talking maybe six or eight years. At least. He's been on a few dates since then, but nothing long-term." She faced Libby. "Is that important to you?"

"I don't know. He seems kind of shy and a little nervous around me. But you and Mike say he's easy-going."

"He is. If he's nervous, it means he's taking a risk."

"With me?"

"I'd say so." Jill appraised her coolly. "Aside from being here tonight, I'd say you're not giving him much encouragement."

Libby leaped to her own defense. "I didn't think I should. It's been—" To her dismay, tears welled in her eyes. She turned away, knotting the dishtowel.

Jill touched her arm gently. "I'm sorry. I guess I was a little protective of Nick there. Are you okay?"

Libby nodded but didn't look at her.

"I've tried to fix Nick up, I don't know how many times," Jill said with a little laugh. "I even thought about your roommate when she came last year."

"Kim?"

"Sure. She's pretty. She seemed a little stand-offish, but I learned she was still in mourning. Nick isn't the man to deal with that. Well, he could be, but he wasn't." She wiped out the sink and said, "Come on, let's go sit down." She took Libby's towel and hung it up, and Libby followed her slowly into the living room.

Jill took a rocking chair, and Libby sat down on the edge of the sofa opposite her.

"I apologize if I've offended you in any way," Jill said. "Mike and I couldn't tell

what was going on. Nick's sat beside you a couple of times at church, and we saw you talking in the parking lot. That's not much in itself, but Sunday night he said some things that made me—both of us—think he's really crazy about you."

Libby opened her mouth and then closed it.

"I was afraid he was going to get hurt," Jill said. "When he asked me to invite you here tonight, I didn't know what to expect. I sort of thought you wouldn't come."

"I almost didn't," Libby admitted.

"Don't you like him?" Jill was clearly anxious.

"Yes, I like him a lot."

When Jill's frown deepened, Libby hovered between telling her everything and keeping silent. She was drawn to Jill and was touched by her obvious love for her brother-in-law.

"I've had what they call a bad experience," she said at last.

Jill rocked her chair slowly back and forth. "A heartbreaking experience?" she asked softly.

"Well, nerve-breaking, at least," Libby said. "I haven't much nerve left when it comes to men, I guess. I've sort of told myself I'd better not date for a while."

"Not a date," Jill said with understanding. "He must have been some creep."

"No, not really. He was very nice. But the ending was fairly traumatic. I didn't feel ready for … Nick."

"Nick is rock solid," Jill said.

Libby cleared her throat. "I thought he deserved something better, something less … tenuous. Someone who hadn't been cauterized emotionally in the last six months. Does that make sense?"

Jill nodded. "In a perverse sort of way. But I think you underestimate Nick."

Libby smiled. "Maybe sometime we could have a cup of tea and I might feel like telling you my tale of woe."

"Yes," said Jill. "When there are no men around."

Libby leaned closer. "Tell me something. You and Mike. Do you pray together?"

"Yes, and we have devotions with the children every evening." Jill seemed surprised at the question.

"Would you pray for me?" Libby watched her face, anxious to have Jill's understanding. "Kim is praying for me, and I'm sure my parents are, but I'd really appreciate it if you would too."

"Of course."

Mike and Nick came noisily in from the garage and splashed in the kitchen sink, washing up. They came into the living room with Joey trailing behind them.

"There you are," said Mike. "Are we going to eat ice cream?"

"Nick, you've got grease on your uniform shirt," Jill scolded. "Make sure your mother sees it. She can probably get it out."

Jill and Libby served dessert, and the Monopoly board came out. Joey played with the adults, counting his money painstakingly. The little girls played with dolls in the bedroom. The game went on until nine o'clock.

"I've got to get Amy to bed," Jill said at last. "Just cash in my deeds. Mike's going to win, anyway." Joey had already gone bankrupt.

"I'm broke," Nick said. "I'll concede."

"Me, too." Libby laid her scant play money beside Mike's much larger pile.

"Well, I appreciate your cooperation," Mike told them. "I told you I'd win at the beginning."

"Yes, you did," said Jill. "You always win. I should know better than to play Monopoly with a businessman."

She got up and went for Amy. Nick brought Libby's coat and Stacy's.

"I'll take you to the car," he said.

Libby turned to Jill. "Thank you so much for inviting me, and—well, for not taking no for an answer."

"Call me," Jill said. "We'll have that cup of tea."

Nick walked out through the garage with Libby, carrying Stacy. He put the little girl into the back seat and fastened the seat belt.

"Thank you, Nick," Libby said. "And thank you for suggesting this. I enjoyed the evening."

He smiled. The half-moon was high above them, and stars glittered in the cold sky. "I thought once you got to know Jill, you'd hit it off."

"We did. I like her a lot."

"So, I'll see you Sunday, I guess."

She nodded.

"I'm supposed to have Sunday off."

Libby said, "You've been really busy this week."

"Yeah, well, it will be worse in November. We're right out straight until deer season ends." He hesitated. "Would you eat lunch with me Sunday?"

She took a deep breath. "Why don't you come to our house? I'm sure Kim won't mind."

He considered. "Okay. Thanks. And thanks for coming tonight."

Libby smiled. "Jill tells me this was not a date, so I guess our record is intact."

He looked a little sheepish. "Maybe I shouldn't have said that to her."

"I said it first." Libby tried to plumb his eyes in the moonlight. "I'm sorry. Maybe I was hasty. I thought I was right to take things slowly, but I think the judgment I made about you was hasty."

He looked across the street, where plastic pumpkins glowed in the yard of Mike and Jill's neighbors. "Well, if you get to where you think a date would be permissible, let me know, okay? Because I think we could have a really nice date if it was in your vocabulary."

"I guess it would be a lot like … tonight?"

He shook his head. "No. No, this wasn't it. This was okay, but a real date would be better. Much better."

Libby chuckled, glancing toward Stacy, who was leaning back against the seat with her eyes closed. "You have a lot of experience in that area?"

"Some. But it's been a while. I would outdo myself if I got the opportunity."

"It's tempting." She saw a smile play at his lips. "I'd better take Stacy home," she said.

Chapter 19

A Huge Mistake

Kim was home when they arrived, and when Stacy was in bed Libby sat down with her roommate and described the evening at the Palmers'.

"It was fun, and you know what?"

"What?" Kim asked, feigning breathlessness.

"I'm contemplating reentering the dating scene."

"Hooray!"

"How about you?" Libby asked.

Kim shook her head. "George called earlier. I told him I wasn't ready."

"Maybe not for marriage, but you could consider going out again."

"We'll see."

***

At ten the next morning, a florist's truck found the isolated farmhouse. Kim took the bouquet in, and Libby and Stacy watched wide-eyed as she laid the box on the table.

"George Franklin is trying to make a last stand?" Libby guessed.

Kim shook her head. "They're for you."

"Me?" Libby lifted the lid cautiously and gasped. She touched the soft petals of a pink rose, and her mouth softened into a smile.

"Here." Kim found the card in its tiny envelope and held it out to her.

Libby opened it, full of anticipation. Her smile crumbled as she read the message, and she let her hand fall to her side.

"What is it?" Kim asked, alarmed.

Libby pulled out a chair and sat down heavily at the kitchen table. She laid the card out where Kim could see it.

Please forgive me. I made a huge mistake. Aiden.

"Oh, boy," said Kim.

"He got the address somewhere. I wouldn't have thought my mother would give it to him."

"Maybe he was very persuasive," Kim speculated. "The flowers are lovely."

Libby got up and walked into the living room and on up the stairs and closed her bedroom door. She sat down on her bed for a minute, then flopped back on her pillow.

Lord, why now? Haven't I been through enough? The tears came, and she prayed for a long time, then wiped her face and put on her jacket and a roll-brim gray hat.

"I'm going for a walk," she said to Kim, as she headed for the carport door. She paused and left her cell phone on the table.

"What if he calls?" Kim asked.

"I'm not home." Libby closed the door firmly behind her.

She walked quickly down the driveway and turned right, away from civilization, along the edge of the tar. A pickup truck with three hunters, resplendent in orange hats and vests, rolled past, but she didn't give it more than a glance.

At the entrance to the gravel pit, she hesitated, listening. There was no sound, and she turned in. The place was deserted. There were more beer cans now, and tire marks where someone had spun circles in the gravel. Several empty shotgun shells lay scattered on the ground, red, yellow, and green, less colorful than the vivid leaves. A few brass casings lay half submerged in the loose soil. She gazed up at the berm. The beech tree held its leaves, but they were completely yellow now. The maple had lost half its foliage and was beginning to look ragged.

She caught her breath. The fox was sprawled lazily on top of a stump, napping in the warm sunshine. Libby thought she'd never seen an animal so cute. Not daring to approach it, she walked slowly to the rock where Nick had set up the targets and pulled herself up on it. She sat for a long time. When it hit her directly, the sun was warm, but then a cloud covered it, and she shivered.

The fox lifted its head and sat still for a moment, sniffing the air. It looked around, and Libby held her breath. The fox pushed up onto its feet and jumped down off the stump. Arching its back, it stretched and then trotted off into the brush. She exhaled, thinking of how she would describe it to Stacy.

A vehicle approached along the road, its engine chugging. It slowed when it got closer. Libby hopped down and walked quickly across to the grassy slope and climbed up beside the maple tree. Before she had quite reached it, a black truck lumbered into the gravel pit and stopped where Nick had parked the week before. There would probably be no trouble, but she should have brought her phone, for safety's sake.

Two men got out, one graying, with glasses and a warm parka. The other was younger, with a beard and a lined denim jacket. Father and son, she surmised, sighting in their rifles for the approaching deer season. She watched as the young man mounted a paper target against the side of the pit, skewering it into place with twigs. When he turned to walk back toward the truck, she shrank against the tree trunk and hoped her drab jacket would camouflage her.

As soon as they began firing their rifles, she walked quickly down the slope toward the road without looking back.

Chapter 20

Avoid Him Forever

"He called," Kim reported, as Libby went through the kitchen door. "You left your phone here, and he called."

Libby gave herself a mental kick. She wouldn't do that to Kim again, going off and leaving her phone behind. That was foolish of her, thinking she could avoid Aiden if he was determined to talk to her.

"He asked when would be a good time to reach you, and I said maybe tonight."

"I won't talk to him." Libby was determined that Aiden would never have a chance to hurt her again.

"You can't avoid him forever," Kim said sadly. "Please don't put me in that position, Libby."

"I'm sorry. I shouldn't have done that." Her friend shouldn't be caught in the maelstrom of her emotional struggles. Libby turned to face her. "Really. I was wrong. Was he rude?"

"No, he was very courteous. He asked if you received flowers, and I said yes. I told him they're beautiful."

Libby didn't say anything, but her thoughts churned.

"He described himself as an old friend."

A bitter laugh escaped Libby. "I thought he was married by now. He should be. Why can't he just leave me alone?"

Her phone was lying on the kitchen table. She picked it up and tapped it for her mother's number, then stretched for the tissue box that sat on the counter. She swiped at a tear as she waited.

"Honey, I'm sorry," Kim said. She looked anxiously at Libby. "I'm taking Stacy outside for a while. She won't be able to play outside much when deer season starts."

Libby nodded and said into the phone, "Hello, Mom? It's me."

"Libby! I'd hoped you were coming down this weekend."

"Did you give Aiden my address and my cell number?" she asked without preliminary.

"Did I …? No, dear. You mean now? No. I haven't heard from him. Has he written to you?"

She sobbed. "He called. I was out. And he sent flowers."

"Oh, my. Maybe he wants to make up," her mother said gently.

"I don't know what he wants, but I'm mad."

"You're upset," Mrs. Sharpe agreed.

"I don't want to talk to him!" Libby slid down to sit on the linoleum.

"You don't have to. But perhaps you should hear him out."

"Why? Why should I?" She lunged for another tissue. "Look, Mom, I can't talk about this right now. I'll call you again sometime." She hung up.

After blowing her nose, she sat gazing across the room at the bouquet of flowers. Kim had arranged them in a vase.

Libby got up slowly and walked over to the table, looking at the perfect roses that were out of season, the ferns and baby's breath. How did he dare think he could make things right so easily? She pulled the bundle of stems from the vase with trembling hands and carried it to the utility room, where she held it deliberately over the trash can and let it fall.

Her phone rang. She turned and glared across the room at it. It might not be him. Kim had told him to call in the evening, and it was not quite noon. She advanced cautiously, and on the fourth ring reached out hesitantly and picked it up. The screen said "Nick."

She exhaled. "Hello?"

"Is that you, Libby?"

"Yes. Hi, Nick."

"Are you all right? You sound a little funny."

"Yes. No." She sighed. The tears were flowing again. She reached for the tissues, plunked the entire box down on the table, and took a seat.

"You don't sound too good," Nick said.

"I'm miserable. You don't want to talk to me right now."

"Why not? What's wrong? Are you sick?"

"No. I'm just ... having a bad day."

"Okay. Should I call another time?"

"No, this is okay. Where are you?"

"Clear up in Dover-Foxcroft, but I figured if I didn't call you now, I might not get a chance."

"What are you doing up there?"

"Oh, someone shot a moose last night, out of season. I don't think we'll find out who did it, but I'll be on duty all day and probably into the evening. I have tomorrow off, though, so I should be able to go to Sunday school."

"That's good." Libby dabbed at her eyes.

"Save me a seat?" he asked.

She smiled. "Yes. I will definitely save you a seat." She sniffed a little.

"Is Kim with you?"

"No, she's outside with Stacy."

"Oh, but she's home?"

"Yes, why?"

"You sound like you're crying, maybe. Are you sure you're all right?"

"I'm feeling a little better now." She wished he didn't know she was upset, but the fact that he had discerned her turmoil comforted her somehow.

"Do you want to talk about it?"

She hesitated. How could she tell him? "I don't think so, but thanks."

"Okay. Maybe Kim, or Jill?"

"Maybe." She sniffed again.

"I better get moving."

"Thanks for calling," Libby said. "You sound just like you on the phone. That's encouraging."

"Well, you don't sound like yourself right now, so maybe I'll check in with you later. Is that okay?"

"Yes," she whispered. "Thank you, Nick."

"Libby." He paused, and she waited, knowing she didn't want the conversation to end. His voice came, so low she could barely hear him. "This doesn't have anything to do with me, does it?"

"No."

"Well, whatever it is that's bothering you, I'll pray for you."

"Thanks. I'll be all right," she said. "I'll talk to you later."

She leaned against the counter for a few seconds after he hung up, then scrolled through her contacts to find Palmer, Michael and Jill.

"Jill, it's Libby. Are you awfully busy?"

"No, what's up?"

"I'm having a bit of a crisis today. Could we have that cup of tea?"

"Sure," Jill said. "Do you want to come here? Or I can come there, if I can bring the girls. Joey is with Mike."

"I'll come there."

Chapter 21

Miles Deep

Libby sat in Jill's kitchen sipping peppermint tea. Jill had made a whole pot, in a white china teapot with daisies on the side. She fed the two little girls their lunch, offering Libby a portion.

"No thanks, but you go ahead," Libby said.

They stayed with church and school chitchat until Rachel and Amy were excused to go and play on the swing set in the backyard.

"So, you come to me with red, puffy eyes and a pocket full of Kleenex," said Jill. "Want to tell me about it?"

Libby nodded. "I guess it's time."

"I'm flattered you came here."

"Well, Kim is really a great friend, but you know Nick so well. I thought maybe you could give me a little of his perspective."

"I'll try. But maybe you should just talk to Nick."

"I can't. Not yet. Not about this." She wiped a tear away. "He called me this morning from Dover-Foxcroft."

"Nick did?"

"Yes."

"That's nice. I mean ... it is, isn't it?"

Libby nodded. "I was really glad he called. I was feeling totally rotten."

Jill poured herself a second cup of tea. "Then it wasn't Nick who made you cry."

"No. Not Nick." Libby looked at Jill through her wet lashes. "Aiden," she said distinctly. "His name is Aiden."

"The man who soured you on dating, I take it?" Jill asked lightly.

"Majorly." Libby held out her teacup, and Jill refilled it. "We were engaged." She lifted the cup to her lips.

"I could have guessed."

"He broke it off at the last minute. June twenty-fifth. That was my wedding day. I spent it packing up all the wedding gifts and writing notes to the people who'd sent them. And crying."

Jill reached out and squeezed her hand. "You're still crying over him?"

"Guess so."

"Is he worth it?"

Libby bit her lip. "This morning a gorgeous bouquet of flowers arrived. I thought it was for Kim at first, from an admirer. She said it was for me, so then I thought Nick had sent it."

"That's not unreasonable, after last night."

Libby gave a bitter little laugh. "I should have known better. I've given Nick the message clearly enough, I guess." She glanced up at Jill, then back at her hands on the cup. She wished Jill had leaped to contradict her. She didn't, so Libby finished, "Aiden sent it."

"Any explanation?"

She pulled the card from the pocket of her jeans and slid it across the tablecloth with one finger. Jill picked it up and read it.

"Hmm."

"I went out to walk, and he called while I was gone. Kim told him to call back tonight." She looked into Jill's eyes pleadingly. "I don't want to talk to him."

Jill thought about it. "Do you think this is an overture, or just an apology?"

"I'm not sure."

112

"Maybe he's truly repentant." Watching Libby carefully, Jill said, "You did love him."

"Did I?"

"You wouldn't commit yourself to a man without love, I'm certain of that." Jill laid the florist's card down on the table between them.

Libby sat for a moment, thinking and looking at the pleasant, sun-washed kitchen. Maybe she'd never really understood what love involved. Had she been close enough to Aiden to realize what was lacking in their relationship? At last she shook her head. "I'd never trust him again."

Jill nodded sympathetically. "Does that mean you can never trust anyone?"

The tears burned in Libby's eyes, and this time she felt a surge of longing, and she knew it was for Nick. "I think I could, after a while." She pulled a tissue out of her pocket. "But it's hard."

Jill waited for her to blow her nose and dump her used tissues in the trash and wash her hands. When Libby sat down again, she said, "Nick is a man who would meet you halfway, Libby."

"Sometimes I think he's warier than I am."

"He's a little scared, I think." Jill smiled. "He hasn't gotten close to a woman for a long, long time. Not since—"

"Not since when?" Libby asked.

Jill shrugged. "It's no secret. I was going to say, not since Diane."

"Diane was his last girlfriend?"

"Oh, he's had dates. But, I think, like you, he'd like to somehow elude the dating process, bypass it completely."

"It gets harder, not easier." Libby sniffed. "So what happened with this Diane?"

"She broke up with him."

"That's it?"

"Well, no, that's an oversimplification."

Libby sipped her tea, thinking about that. What sort of

113

woman had Nick chosen? And why had she rejected him? "Was she pretty?" she asked at last.

"You've seen her."

Libby stared at Jill in disbelief. "I have? Diane?" Her brain quickly catalogued every Diane she'd ever met. But it had to be someone here, in the Waterville area. "Not Diane Griffin!"

"Yes, well, Diane Folsom she was then."

Libby tried to absorb that, picturing Drew and Diane Griffin at church, their little boy between them in the pew. "So you're saying Nick used to date Diane, but she broke up with him and married Drew, and he's had to see them at church two or three times a week for all these years?"

Jill shrugged. "He came to terms with it a long time ago. He could have gone to another church, I guess, or just quit going, but he didn't. Nick's not that kind of man."

"He just faces up to things?" Libby said.

"Yes."

"When was all this?"

"He started dating her in high school. He went to UMaine, and she went off to school, out of state. He wrote to her faithfully. The second year, the letters kind of petered out, I guess. When they were home at Christmas that year, he wasn't happy, but they still saw each other. By spring it was over. Diane came home and had a job at the grocery store that summer. She started going out with Drew. She didn't go back to school in the fall."

"What did Nick do?"

"Just kept on working and going to school. Drew and Diane got married that April."

"Nick was at school?"

"He came home weekends. He went to the wedding."

"How could he?" She tried to see herself attending Aiden's wedding without breaking down. Impossible.

Jill shook her head. "He's miles deep."

Libby took a deep breath. "Makes me feel kind of shallow."

Jill smiled. "This Aiden. If he calls, just tell him how you feel."

"I will." If Nick could do it, she could too. She would tell Aiden in no uncertain terms that she wanted nothing further to do with him.

"And one more thing," Jill said, rising and looking out the laundry room window toward the swing set, where Rachel and Amy sat opposite each other on the chair swing. "If Nick calls again ..."

"Yeah?"

Jill sat back down across from Libby. "Tell him how you feel too. Don't keep him guessing."

Libby smiled. "Thanks. I'd better get home. I was going to do a lot of work today, getting things ready for school, and I've wasted most of it. But sometime I want you to tell me how you and Mike got together."

Jill laughed. "It's not a long story. We were both business majors, met in the computer lab, and couldn't take our eyes off each other."

Chapter 22

The Black Knight

Kim was concerned when Libby arrived home.

"Did you and Jill Palmer talk things out?"

"Yes, a little. Thank you." Libby smiled at Kim, knowing her eyes were still red-rimmed. "Kim, you're such a good friend." She reached out and hugged her housemate. "I'll be here all evening if any gentlemen should call."

"Good."

"Would you pray about this with me?" Libby asked. "I'm still nervous about Aiden coming back into my life."

"Of course."

It was seven o'clock when he phoned. Kim had just turned off the TV, after the news broadcast. She looked questioningly at Libby. Libby picked up her cell and walked slowly to the kitchen.

"Hello?"

"Libby! It's so good to hear your voice."

She breathed, deeply and slowly. "Aiden."

"I want to talk to you, Libby. Can I see you?"

She was frightened suddenly. How could he think he might see her, if he were in Kentucky? "Where are you?"

"I'm in Boston. It's not so far."

"It's too far. Four hours or so."

"I'll leave now if you say the word."

She was silent for a moment. "No, I don't think so."

"I have to be back in Louisville Monday, but I'm determined to resolve this thing now, this weekend."

"It was resolved in June, Aiden. There are no loose ends."

"I disagree. Please let me come up there. Or meet me in Portland."

"No." She said it quietly, firmly. She turned toward the living room, where Kim came to lean against the doorjamb. She eased close enough to reach for Kim's hand. Kim squeezed her fingers and smiled.

"Libby, I was so wrong," Aiden said. "I never should have done what I did. I want to make it up to you. I'll do anything—"

"No," she said again, firmer. Kim gave her the thumbs up sign.

"Libby, I love you."

Libby was quiet.

"Are you there?" he asked.

"Yes. It's awfully difficult to believe that, Aiden. The last time I saw you, you said you were mistaken. It wasn't love, it was a lengthy infatuation. Your exact words."

Kim smiled just a little, then moved away from the doorway, and Libby heard the stairs creak.

"Libby, that was—I was so confused. Please give me a chance to explain."

"I don't think I really want to go into it."

"Please—"

"Just tell me one thing," she said. "How did you get my address and telephone number?"

"From the college alumni office."

She sighed. It was that easy for him. So much for student confidentiality.

"I thought you were getting married," she said.

"I—no. That was incorrect information you received. Disseminated prematurely."

"Oh, brother. You talk eduspeak now, Aiden." She used to think his way of speaking was a part of his sophistication. Now he just sounded arrogant.

"Libby, I'll be there by eleven. I have a map. Just tell me what exit for I-95."

"Forget it. I don't want to see you." She stabbed at the screen to close the connection.

Almost immediately the phone rang. He couldn't call back that fast. She swiped the screen cautiously.

"Elizabeth?"

"Nick," she breathed with relief.

"Yes. You sound better."

She laughed. "I feel better. I just did something that took fortitude. Resolution. Valor, even."

"I'm intrigued."

"I'd like to tell you about it sometime."

"I'd like to hear it."

"Maybe after lunch tomorrow? Kim and Stacy are really glad you're coming to lunch. So am I." Across the miles, she could almost see his sparkling brown eyes.

"So, maybe after lunch you could tell me about your deeds of valor."

"I'll try. And if I should cry, you would understand that when a woman commits an act of courage, sometimes she collapses in tears when it's over? It wouldn't be anything personal."

"Since you've warned me, I guess I could keep that in mind."

"Good, because I've gone through a lot of tissues today, and I'd hate to get weepy on you without you knowing why."

"This is purely a gender thing?"

"Pretty much. I don't think the vanquished party is in tears right now."

"So, you've vanquished a challenger?"

"The Black Knight." Libby tossed her hair back.

"Yup, I really want to hear that story," Nick said. "But for now, farewell, sweet lady. I must return to my quest."

"Many thanks, kind sir, for conveying your sentiments."

***

Nick couldn't help smiling as he went back to Tom Hatfield's car.

"Make your phone call?" Tom asked.

"Yup. You want to call Debbie?"

"No, she'll expect me when she sees me." Tom put the car in gear and headed out for the long ride home. Darkness had fallen, and he scanned the road ahead, alert for deer or moose in the right of way. He glanced at Nick. "You look happy."

"I guess I am," Nick admitted. The smile could not be subdued.

"Must be a girl," Tom grunted.

Nick's smile broadened.

"Quite a girl," Tom revised.

"Yeah, she really is."

"Anyone I know?"

He hesitated. Would Libby be upset if she knew he was talking about her with Tom? He wanted to tell everyone that he was seeing Libby Sharpe, and let all his friends share his delight.

"You remember the teacher?"

"What teacher? Mrs. Richardson?"

"Yes. It's her roommate. Libby Sharpe."

"Never did get a look at her," Tom replied.

"She's worth a look," Nick said, and was immediately appalled at himself.

Tom smiled knowingly. "So, you've finally got a woman in your life. About time."

Yes, thought Nick. *It is time.* God's timing, he was certain.

He had wondered all day what or who had made Libby cry, and sent up a hundred short, fervent prayers for her. There was a man involved. All right, so be it. He'd figured that was the case, since the day they shot cans together in the gravel pit. He hadn't been sure whether her self-imposed ban on dating was because she loved another man, or because she hated one. But there had to be a man.

She'd said he was gone now, out of the picture. And she wasn't crying anymore. Maybe there weren't any pieces to pick up, but he was ready if she needed him.

Chapter 23

Windmills or Windbags

Libby slept soundly. The pulp truck failed to waken her at dawn Sunday, but the alarm clock came through at seven thirty, and she sprang out of bed and went to the kitchen, where she began making lasagna.

When she had put it, unbaked, in the refrigerator, she woke Stacy and Kim, and the three of them ate breakfast and tidied up the house in anticipation of their company.

At nine, Kim shooed Libby off to dress and took Stacy in hand. Libby meticulously prepared for church, choosing a warm blue velour dress and black shoes. She pulled the top of her hair back in a silver barrette and hooked a silver chain, her parents' gift on her college graduation, around her neck.

A knock on her door heralded Stacy's arrival for inspection.

"Aunt Libby, you look beautiful," Stacy declared.

"So do you." Libby smiled and stooped for a hug.

"Your dress feels like a kitten," Stacy squealed.

The little girl was wearing her favorite color again, a purple corduroy jumper over a print turtleneck, and cable knit white tights.

They joined Kim and put on their coats.

"Thirty-nine degrees," said Kim. "Pretty chilly."

"Could be worse," Libby countered.

When they got to the church, she looked around the

parking lot for Nick's truck, but didn't see it or the Explorer. They went inside, and Kim deposited Stacy in the 4's and 5's class, then rejoined Libby in the adult class in the auditorium, two thirds of the way back, with an empty spot on the aisle for Nick.

Mike and Jill Palmer stopped beside their pew to say hello.

"How you doing?" Jill asked, giving Libby's hand a squeeze.

"Much better, thank you." In a near whisper, she added, "I think I survived the challenge last night."

"Good for you! Tell me about it sometime." Jill and Mike sat down in the pew ahead of Kim and Libby. One of the deacons, Howard Banks, stood up to begin the class.

Behind her, the auditorium doors opened and closed softly several times. Libby made herself not look back, but when Nick slipped into the aisle seat, she turned her smile on him for an instant, and met an exultant look. She didn't think the joy could be sustained undiluted for forty-five minutes, but she never became less aware of it as the class progressed.

When the lesson ended, she turned toward Nick. His eyes locked hers, and her stomach lurched.

"How's everything?" he asked.

"Great."

"I'm glad." His eyes said much more than the terse reply, and Libby decided conciseness was a virtue. She wondered how much her eyes were telling him. His smile deepened, and she was certain he was seeing something there that pleased him.

"Hey, Nicky," his brother said, turning around in the pew. "How you doing?"

Nick shook Mike's hand heartily. "Terrific."

Libby became aware that Jill was watching her watch Nick, and she turned away quickly, her cheeks warm.

Jill leaned toward her and whispered, "I think progress has been made."

Libby smiled, lowering her eyes.

Joey and Rachel came to sit with their parents, and Joey turned around to have a word with Uncle Nick.

"Are you coming to our house today?"

"Not today, buddy."

"Oh, come on."

"Another time."

The choir filed in on the platform, and Pastor Wilson and the song leader sat down in chairs behind the pulpit. Mike tapped Joey on the shoulder and told him to turn around, and a hush moved over the room.

***

Lunch was a great success, in Nick's opinion. After he had filled himself with Libby's lasagna and Kim's peanut butter pie, he suggested a walk for himself and Libby, to burn off some of the calories. It was as good an excuse as any. He wanted to talk to Libby alone, and he knew that both she and Kim knew that.

The air was warmer now, and Libby changed her shoes, pulling a gray fleece jacket over her dress, and put on her hat. The saucy rolled brim made her look about sixteen, and full of mischief as she smiled up at him with just a trace of timidity. Nick pulled on his light jacket, with a quilted vest over it.

"Where do you want to go?" he asked, as they went out through the carport. He heard distant gun shots. "Sounds like someone's shooting in the gravel pit."

"They've been doing a lot of that this weekend," Libby said.

"Well, it's a safe place to practice. Opening day is Saturday for residents."

"I hope the fox is okay. I saw it yesterday." She glanced up at him.

He smiled, warm inside, knowing he'd introduced her to the critter.

"How about we go down the lane?" Libby asked.

"All right, but after Friday you don't want to come out here without wearing orange," Nick warned. "That's a pretty big patch of woods, and there'll be hunters in there for sure."

They walked leisurely down the farm lane, past the swing set and the old apple trees behind the house, to the edge of the woods.

"What kind of tree is that?" Nick asked, pointing to one with tan, peeling bark.

Libby peered closely and said, "Yellow birch."

"A-plus," said Nick. She had been doing her homework. It pleased him inordinately that she'd taken the tree study seriously.

An overgrown trail continued at the end of the lane, heading into the woods. "Ever go back here?"

"No. Kim says this path used to go to the river, but it's all brush now."

Nick pushed aside an overhanging pine branch and said, "Let's see." The path was discernible enough to be inviting, but sufficiently overgrown to lend an air of past secrets waiting to be discovered.

They walked along, sidestepping bushes and brambles. After fifty feet, it was hard to distinguish the trail. A large rock pushed up through the turf beside the path, and Nick was doubtful they could go much farther without difficulty. He nodded toward the rock. "Want to sit here and talk?" He took off his vest and laid it on the rock.

Libby smiled and sat down on the vest.

Nick sat beside her, bracing his feet on the ground below the rock. He folded his arms and looked at her expectantly.

"So, you've tilted at windmills."

"Or windbags," Libby said.

He laughed, and her face reddened.

"I shouldn't say that. He isn't really a windbag. I've just been mad at him so long!"

"How long?"

"Four months, at least."

"Not so long," Nick said carefully. He remembered when Diane had broken up with him. He'd agonized for a lot longer than that, trying to see what he'd done wrong.

"Long enough, I think," Libby said determinedly. "I'm done stewing about it."

He watched her face intently. "Who is this Black Knight who had such awesome power over you?"

"My fiancé."

Nick raised his eyebrows. It was a bit of a surprise. A boyfriend, he'd expected. This was far more serious than he'd supposed. But she couldn't have been engaged when she came to Waterville. He unfolded his arms and reached across, picking up her left hand gently and scrutinizing it. He shook his head. "No ring."

"Correction," said Libby. "My former fiancé."

"Ah." He settled back on the rock, folding his hands together in his lap and looking at her with anticipation. As long as everything was in the past, he knew he could handle the feelings it would bring. There was bound to be at least a faint jealousy, and, depending on how badly the fellow had treated her, anger, disgust, or sorrow.

Libby swallowed hard. "We were engaged to be married last June." She saw no change in Nick's expression. "The wedding date was … June twenty-fifth. Are you sure you want to hear this?" Anxiety was creeping into her voice.

"I want to hear it very much."

Chapter 24

The Awkwardness Factor

Libby gazed at Nick's strong, angular jaw and his firm mouth, straight nose, and clear, compelling brown eyes.

"He broke up with me," she raised her hands in a gesture of helplessness. "I was very hurt, but somehow, I wasn't surprised."

"No?"

"All along I'd felt it wasn't real somehow."

"In what way?"

Nick's dark eyes were patient but unrelenting, and she knew she had to continue. She owed him that.

"We were apart most of our engagement. He was teaching in Kentucky. I had a contract in Gorham when we got engaged. It was a year ago, in late August. He wanted me to quit then, but I felt I should stay the school year." She shook her head, stroking the soft heads of moss that clung to the side of the rock. "If I'd done what he wanted, none of this would have happened."

"I'm glad it happened," Nick said quite fiercely, and she looked up in surprise. He was still watching her intently.

After letting that sink in, she was unable to keep a smile from forming on her lips. "I guess I am, too, but I never was before. It didn't seem like something to be glad about. It was a tragedy. A bitter disappointment."

"God has something else for you," he said, and her heart

leaped. "Was this man a Christian?"

"Yes, he was. Is. I don't think he intended to hurt me. But we were apart so long." She looked up at him, searching for support.

"Stop now, or you'll be saying it was all your fault," Nick said.

"Well, he didn't want to wait the whole school year."

"So. It would be a small price to pay, to have the rest of his life with … you."

She thought about that, trying to ignore the shiver of excitement Nick's implication sent through her. At the time, she had thought her decision to wait through the school year had been reasonable, and Aiden had reluctantly agreed. But later, when he'd told her the wedding was off, she was convinced she had been foolish and demanding.

"Where's the ring?" Nick asked.

Her gaze snapped up to his. "I mailed it back in June. I figured another girl was wearing it now, but then, yesterday—"

"You went to the lists yesterday and emerged triumphant."

She smiled and looked down at her hands. "He sent flowers."

Nick was silent.

"There was a card. It said, *Please forgive me. I made a huge mistake.*" She looked anxiously at him but saw no change except a slight lowering of his eyebrows. "I cried," she confessed.

"I know. When I talked to you yesterday, I could tell."

Libby swallowed. Had she cried for the loss of Aiden, or for something else? "I went to see Jill, and she was very helpful. Gave me some perspective."

"I'm glad," Nick said. "You two are a lot alike."

"Well, Aiden called last night, just before you did," Libby revealed in a small voice.

"We get to the jousting at last."

"Yes."

"Did you knock him off his high horse?"

She smiled. "I'm not sure. But I told him I didn't want to see him."

"He wanted to come up here? From Kentucky?"

"He said he was in Boston for the weekend, and that he would drive up. I put the kibosh on that."

"Did he say why he wanted to come?"

She writhed slightly, thinking about what little she had let Aiden say. "He wanted to talk. Thought he could—make it up to me—somehow." A red squirrel ran up the trunk of an oak on the other side of the path and scampered out on a branch, chattering at them.

"So, you told him it's over."

"I told him it was over in June, and there's no question of the fat lady singing now. Or something like that."

Nick laughed. He reached for her hand and clasped it in his, and Libby felt a renewed conviction that she had done the right thing, and that she wanted Nick Palmer in her life.

"Elizabeth, that makes me very happy." He sobered and said, "Would you consider revisiting the topic of first dates?"

Solemnly, Libby watched the little squirrel as he hung from the branch by his front paws, then regained his balance. She struggled for her own equilibrium. "I guess I'd consider it now, but Jill says both of us are trying to figure out how to bypass the dating process."

He chuckled. "I guess you and Jill did have a heart-to-heart." He tightened his hold on her hand. "How about Friday night? It's the only night before hunting season starts that's not a school night for you. After deer season opens, I may not have an evening free all month."

"All right, I accept."

"Really?"

Libby had never seen such joy in Aiden's eyes, even when she'd finally accepted his marriage proposal. Satisfaction, yes. Elation, no. But Nick was definitely elated, and it made her heart sing.

"You know," she said, "for the last four months, I've had a

real struggle, trying to be thankful to God, and not ever really being able to feel that way."

"And now?"

She tipped her head back and looked up at the cerulean sky, high above the yellow and orange and green treetops.

"Now I'm very grateful. God had to bring me here in tears. He gave me a job, a home, friends, a great church, everything I needed, and I was still unthankful."

"You weren't looking at the big picture," Nick said.

"Sometimes my emotions get in the way, I guess."

"So, we'll have our first date on Friday?"

She smiled up at him. "Yes, I think we're ready."

"Unless you want to skip the first one."

She frowned. "Well, first dates are usually pretty awkward."

Nick said pensively, "Maybe the awkwardness factor for a first date is inversely proportional to the number of non-dates experienced before the actual event." He looked at her solemnly.

Libby tried to keep a straight face but ended up laughing. She squeezed his hand. "You pick the time and the place and let me know."

"All right, but if you get nervous, we'll just call it our second date and take it from there." He stood up, pulling her to her feet, and picked up his vest. They walked hand in hand, back along the overgrown path, turning sideways to skirt an aggressive blackberry bush with scarlet leaves.

They emerged into the field at the end of the lane and ambled on to the house. As they rounded the corner of the carport, Nick glanced down the driveway and said, "Looks like you've got company."

Chapter 25

Just Be Here

A red Camaro was parked in the driveway behind Kim's Saturn and Nick's truck.

"I don't know this car," Libby said. "It must be a friend of Kim's."

"Massachusetts plate," observed Nick. "Could be a rental." He eyed her carefully.

Libby stopped, dropping his hand, staring at the car. "No, he wouldn't! Would he?" Dismayed, she turned to Nick.

"The Black Knight?" he asked.

"It's him! I told him not to come."

Nick glanced toward the house then pulled her back behind the wall of the carport. "Libby, if you don't want to see him, I can take care of that."

"How?"

"Just stay out here, out of sight. I'll go in and tell him."

"What would you tell him?" Libby's lips trembled. "You can't lie to him."

"I wouldn't," Nick said, capturing her hand again. "I'd tell him that you don't want to see him and he should leave."

She searched his features, trying to excavate his deepest feelings. "No. I've got to face him and send him away myself. It's not your job, Nick."

"I could take this on for you." She could see that he truly longed to do it, to champion her, to keep her from an ugly scene, and to show her how much he cared about her.

She shook her head. "Thank you, no. But please, Nick, don't go away."

"What do you want me to do?"

"Just be here."

He put his hands on her shoulders. "All right. Libby, I'll be right here with you. And I'll follow your lead. If you want to use me, do it. Tell him I'm part of your life now. Tell him I'm wild about you, and I'm committed to you, that you're the bright spot in my life, and that's not going to change. Tell him I will never break up with you like he did, or expect you to send back a symbol of my love for you—"

She put her fingers up to his lips to stop the flow of words. "Nick, I can't. I won't lie to make it easier."

"It wouldn't be a lie." He was earnest, unflinching, confident. She sensed with awe that he hadn't planned to pour out his heart so soon, but if circumstances called for it, he was ready. His deep brown eyes pleaded with her. "Just don't give him any ground, Libby. Not one inch. Please."

She forced her gaze away from his and looked back toward the edge of the forest, where the hardwoods flamed and the evergreens stood cool and dark. Her voice cracked a little when she said, "Nick, you can't tell me things like that and expect me to go in there calm and efficient. That's what I need, to do this job."

"All right." He heaved a sigh and stood looking down at her for a long moment. At last he said quietly, "Let's pray just for a minute, before we go in."

She bowed her head, and Nick bent toward her, letting his forehead rest against hers, below the brim of her soft hat. His skin was cool, and she stood still under his touch, waiting without question as he asked the Lord for wisdom, strength, and courage for them both.

"I won't go in unless you want me to," he said when he had finished.

"Thank you. I want you there. Just let me do the talking,

please, unless I ask you to." A grim determination buttressed her eagerness to have the matter over with at last.

He nodded gravely, and she strode toward the house with Nick beside her.

They were sitting in the living room. Kim jumped up as Libby opened the kitchen door and walked briskly into the room.

"Libby, there you are!" Her eyes were expressive, telegraphing news of the visitor.

"I saw the car," Libby said softly. She walked resolutely toward the living room doorway. Stacy was seated on the couch, still in her purple jumper, staring soberly at the tall, blond man who had risen to his feet from the armchair. Aiden.

Libby couldn't help contrasting him with Nick. Height was about the same for the two, but Aiden's light hair was wavy, and his nose thin with a slight bend in the middle. He wore metal-framed glasses, and his chin was a little pointed. He looked like an academic, and his tweed jacket, brown knit vest and checked shirt continued the theme.

She wished Nick was wearing his uniform, until she glanced around at him and saw him standing, solid and supportive, behind her. His attitude was uncompromising, and his dark hair and eyebrows were emphatically natural, like his temperament. She knew that if she were a step closer, she would smell the woods on him, and the clean, chill air that was almost November.

"Libby, at last!" Aiden reached out with both hands, and she stopped in her tracks, not wanting to touch him. He advanced anyway, grasped one of her hands, and leaned toward her, aiming for her right cheek.

Libby took a step back to avoid his kiss and bumped into Nick, who put his hands on the back of her jacket to steady her momentarily and stepped back a little himself.

"Please don't, Aiden," Libby said. "If you want to talk, we'll sit down for a few minutes, but I've really said all I want to say. I told you not to come."

Chapter 26

Immovable

Kim edged past Nick and said quietly, "Stacy, come with Mommy." She took Stacy to the kitchen, and they heard the refrigerator door open.

"All right," Aiden said with forced pleasantry, "we'll sit." He took the armchair, and Libby moved to the couch and eased down, relieved when Nick sat beside her.

There were empty cups on the coffee table. "Would you like more coffee?" Libby asked.

"No, thank you. I've had plenty. Your roommate has been entertaining me for the last thirty minutes." Libby squirmed under his suggestion that it was her fault, and that spending a half hour with Kim was a waste of his precious time.

Aiden fixed his gaze on Nick with instant dislike.

"This is Nicholas Palmer." Libby flicked a glance toward him. "Nick, this is Aiden Knight."

Nick showed just a hint of a smile when she made the introduction. "Mr. Knight." His voice was lazy, but Libby could feel his tension.

She plunged into the morass. "Aiden, I asked you not to come here. I meant it."

"I needed to see you. I couldn't express what I wanted to say over the phone. Libby, that's part of what went wrong before, don't you see? We weren't able to express our true thoughts and feelings in person. Long distance communications just don't work in some situations."

His plea didn't cause her feelings to waver, and she said quietly, "I thought you made it excruciatingly clear last June. There was no doubt of your thoughts and feelings."

Aiden sighed and turned his head to one side, then faced her again. "May I speak with you alone, please?"

"No."

Nick's shoulder brushed against hers. He had leaned imperceptibly toward her until their sleeves touched, and the warmth of it gave her a rush of confidence.

Aiden sat in silence, projecting a challenge across the coffee table. Libby didn't move or speak. At last, he said, "You're not being fair, Libby."

Nick stirred beside her, and she said quickly, "Life is not fair, Aiden. Was it fair when you promised me marriage and a home and undying devotion, then whisked it all away without explanation, except that you were 'having doubts'?"

He leaned forward, ignoring Nick. "I admit I needed some time to think things through, but Libby, you took over a year to decide you would accept my suit in the first place. Now I've taken four months to reconsider, and I've decided that I love you and I want to continue our relationship. Is that so unbalanced? I gave you time, even when you insisted on moving back to New England. Now you begrudge me four months?"

His argument struck her as absurd. Libby gave a tight little laugh. "You never asked me for time. You said it was over. You *broke* the engagement, Aiden. You didn't just stick it in the freezer for a while."

His face reddened. "I am serious here. Please don't be flippant. I came all the way—"

She jumped up, and the two men automatically stood too. "No, Aiden, I don't want to listen to this. And don't try to tell me there wasn't another woman in this, because I have impeccable sources."

That hit home. His jaw dropped, but nothing came out.

She'd known it. Her old college friend had written in distress, but Libby had made sure of her facts.

"Excuse me. This interview is over. Please leave." She walked past Nick and up the stairs, forbidding herself to run or to cry in Aiden's presence.

***

Aiden stood by the armchair looking after her, his face a blank, then turned around to appraise Nick. Raising his chin a fraction of an inch, Nick met his gaze calmly.

Kim came uncertainly to the doorway and looked in at them.

"I suppose you are the cause of this tantrum," Aiden said, eyeing Nick distastefully.

He chuckled. "No, you are. Elizabeth has asked you to leave, Mr. Knight. Please comply with her wishes."

The two stood unmoving for several seconds. Nick knew he could stand motionless in the woods for hours when he was hunting, and he could stand here as long as necessary, immovable. He doubted Aiden Knight had ever developed the skill. After ten seconds, Knight turned away abruptly, a red stain in his cheeks. He strode toward the kitchen, and Kim dodged hastily out of the doorway.

"Good-bye," said Stacy, who sat at the table eating graham crackers and milk.

Knight walked out the door without a reply, and the Camaro's engine started. Nick watched out the window until the red car was gone then turned to Kim.

"Would you mind telling Elizabeth that the coast is clear?"

Kim smiled, and Nick smiled back.

"With pleasure." Kim skipped up the stairs and returned with a subdued Libby.

Nick met her at the bottom of the staircase, his heart brimming with relief and love. Libby put her hand on his sleeve and said simply, "Thank you."

"I didn't do much." He shrugged, but his heart was pounding.

"Yes, you did." Libby's smile was grateful and knowing. "I need to do some thinking about a lot of things that were said today." Her brown eyes beseeched him to be patient without branding her unfair or capricious.

He looked over his shoulder. Kim had gone into the kitchen and was taking Stacy's glass to the sink.

"All right," he said, "but if you can't remember some of them, or need to hear anything repeated, I'm a pretty good witness. Especially when it comes to my own testimony."

She nodded. "I don't think I'll forget it."

Chapter 27

Hurricane Jade

Nick was waiting in the church's frosty parking lot when Kim pulled her Saturn into a slot that evening. Libby tried to breathe slowly and evenly so her heart wouldn't gallop away.

With Kim's permission, he got Stacy out of the back seat and carried her in, even though she was awake. They sat in the next to the last pew with Nick on the aisle, and Libby felt she had a brick wall at her back, something permanent that would shield her and support her.

"Let me take you home," he said afterward, as they walked down the steps.

She hesitated.

"We'll follow Kim," he said. "It will give me ten minutes to talk to you."

She capitulated, and he put Stacy in Kim's car and came to open the truck door for her.

"I may not see you again until Friday night," he told her in his truck. "I'll try to be here Wednesday night for prayer meeting, but I don't know if it will happen. I wanted to clarify something."

"All right." Libby watched his hands as he adjusted the defroster and steered into the roadway. Unless she was badly mistaken, his feelings were clear now.

"I meant the things I said today. About how I feel." He glanced her way, but the darkness concealed his expression. "I realize it was a panic-induced declaration, and it may have been too soon for you to hear some of that."

"Nick, we haven't even had our first date," she said gently.

"We're way past that, Libby—dates or no dates. I feel very strongly about you. I know you're still dealing with the fallout from the Black Knight, but I want to be part of your life permanently. If you'll let me, I'll always be there for you. I'll—"

"Nick, please. Let me get used to you driving me home from church and calling me sporadically and maybe holding my hand once in a while."

"Is that all?" he asked.

"For now. For this week, anyway." She needed a time of definition. She couldn't oust Aiden from her heart and immediately fill it with Nick. The old custom of observing a mourning period seemed sensible to her for the first time. She needed to know, once and for all, that the past was past.

"All right." He fell silent. As the truck sped along Kennedy Drive, he reached over and folded her hand in his and held it firmly. Libby started to pull away gently but changed her mind. His hand was large and warm and extremely reassuring. Amazed, she found herself returning the small pressure he gave her hand, and his smile deepened.

She didn't say anything until he stopped in her driveway and came around to open the door for her. She hadn't been very gracious, and she found she wanted to encourage him, no matter what she had declared a week before. Her future without Nick would be bleak and empty.

As she climbed down from the cab, the wind whipping her hair, she said, "I have all kinds of feelings too, Nick. I'm not trying to be mysterious or anything."

He smiled, glancing ahead to where Kim and Stacy were closing the Saturn's doors. "So, sometime you'll tell me what they are?" He put his left hand on the back of her jacket as they approached the steps.

"Yes," Libby said. "When I've mustered my courage

again."

He nodded. "I can wait. Button up tonight," he said, louder, including Kim. "Hurricane Jade is coming up the coast, and the tail end will probably hit us soon."

***

Libby and Kim drew water in pitchers and pans and set out candles and matches on the counter. After midnight, Libby awoke to rain drumming on the roof. She got up to watch out the window as the wind tore leaves from the trees. They swirled over the lawn like pale night birds, swooping about, searching in vain for their nests. She wondered where the deer were bedded down and hoped the fox was snug in his den.

The next morning, she drove to school through puddles of standing water, amazed at the number of trees standing bare now, finger-like twigs scratching toward the gray sky.

Kim had after-school duty that day, and Libby stayed in her classroom, preparing for the week ahead. As they drove home in twilight, the wind still gusted, shoving at the car, nudging it toward the shoulder. As soon as they got home, they drew more water.

"Get your flashlight," Kim advised. "If we lose power tonight, you'll need it."

"What do we do for heat if that happens?" Libby asked.

Kim frowned. "Well, there's an old wood stove down in the basement, but that's a last resort. I think I'd go to the pastor's first."

Stacy found the entire event exciting, even though the electricity didn't fail. They laid out their clothes for the next day and breakfast things that needed no cooking. The rain pounded the roof in the night, louder now, and then gentle for a while, but constant.

The storm continued through Tuesday, and the wind buffeted the students as they ran from buses and cars to the school door. Teachers took turns organizing games in the gymnasium during the lunch hour.

Libby dragged home tired that evening. As she dried their supper dishes, the lights flickered and went out, the refrigerator stopped humming, and the clothes dryer stopped abruptly without its usual buzz. They spent the evening huddled in the living room wrapped in afghans, playing Parcheesi with Stacy by candlelight. Their cell phones still worked, and Nick called at seven thirty, asking if they had power.

"No, we're in the Dark Ages," Libby said.

"Do you have everything you need?"

"Well, it's chilly here, but I think we'll be all right tonight."

"It's not supposed to freeze," Nick said.

She told him about the wood stove in the cellar.

"I could maybe come by later and get it going for you." Libby turned him down, and he said he would check in with her the next day.

They went to bed early to save the candles, piling extra quilts on their beds. Kim took Stacy into her bed with her. Libby lay awake, hearing the gale swirl around the old house, rattling the windows and searching for loose shingles.

Chapter 28

Strength Every Day

When the pulp truck rumbled past, Libby awoke shivering. She reached for her Bible and flashlight and read her morning devotions curled up in a ball under four blankets. At six o'clock, she heard Kim's phone ringing faintly from the room across the hall. Before Libby could force herself out of her nest, her housemate knocked on her door.

"School's canceled. No power at the school."

"Well, it's too cold to stay here," Libby said.

Kim opened her door a crack and stuck her head in. "Should we evacuate, or call Nick?"

Libby hesitated. "Shouldn't we be able to start that stove ourselves?"

"Have you ever used a wood stove?"

"No."

"Well, I have, but it's been years," Kim eyed her doubtfully.

In the end, they dressed in multiple sweaters and took flashlights to the cellar, leaving Stacy huddled in Kim's bed.

Kim inspected the stovepipe that went into the chimney then began building her pile of tinder and kindling in the firebox. She sent Libby scrambling for old newspaper and had her tear pieces of bark from sticks of birch that were part of their meager firewood supply.

A hatchet lay beside the old woodbox, and Kim used it to

cleave slivers of wood from one of the split birch logs. At last she set a match to the bottom of the little pile. They blew on the flame and watched hopefully as the bark and sticks began to blaze.

"Hooray," Kim cried, adding small sticks. "It will be a while before we feel the heat upstairs, but if we take care of this fire, we should be warm before too long."

They treated the day as a holiday, and Stacy reveled in helping Libby mount pictures of twins for her November bulletin boards. Mrs. Mitchell had given Libby several back issues of *Twins* magazine, and they were full of attractive photos. Libby planned to read the Biblical account of the twins Jacob and Esau the first day and discuss fraternal and identical twins with her students.

By ten o'clock, the lower rooms of the house were comfortable, and Kim decided to heat soup for lunch on the wood stove. They spent a lazy afternoon in reading and mending. Kim brought out her workbag and added to an afghan she was making as a Christmas gift for her grandmother, and she set Stacy to work, crocheting an endless length of chain stitches.

The sun went down too fast. They dressed for prayer meeting early, to avoid lighting the candles until it was necessary, then ate a supper of sandwiches, juice from a bottle, and leftover cookies. Kim loaded the stove and nearly closed the damper before they left. The wind had abated, but the rain still fell, gently now.

A soggy cardboard sign was tacked to the church door, lettered with permanent marker: "Prayer meeting at the parsonage." They ran toward the pastor's house, trying to avoid puddles.

Pastor and Sarah Wilson welcomed them into their living room, where a box stove radiated heat and two kerosene lamps brightened the cream walls and blue print sofa and armchair, the walnut piano and overflowing bookshelves. Old Mrs. Childs and the Perkins family were seated there, discussing the weather and ways they were coping with the blackout.

"I don't expect many out tonight," said the pastor, "but if we get many more, we'll need more chairs."

There was seating enough for Kim, Libby, and Stacy, but soon afterward the Palmer family followed. Mike carried Amy in, and Jill held an umbrella over herself and Rachel. Joey came in the door crying and dripping wet, holding out to Libby a soggy piece of paper.

"Miss Sharpe, I'm sorry," he sobbed.

"What is it, Joey?" Libby took the paper from his hand and wiped the rain and tears from his face.

"He went splat in a puddle and dropped Nick's note," Mike said. "He was so proud of being responsible for it that he forgot to watch where his feet were going."

"Oh, honey, it's all right, I can still read it." Libby carefully unfolded the single sheet. "See, it says, *Elizabeth— Going to Madison. Lost hunter. Call on Mike or Pastor if you need anything. N.P.* I can still read it just fine."

Joey sniffed and said solemnly, "N.P. is my Uncle Nick."

Libby reached out and hugged him. "I know. Thank you very much for bringing me this." Her skirt was wet from Joey's soaked clothing, and Mrs. Wilson brought him a throw to wrap around himself. The Palmer children sat on the floor, and Stacy joined them while Mike and Jill found seats.

The group prayed together, praising God for His majesty and enumerating prayer requests, including those without electricity who were shivering in their dark homes that night, and a force of game wardens, state troopers, and citizens in Madison thirty miles away, searching the woods for a fifty-year-old man who had gone out to shoot partridge that afternoon and hadn't come home.

***

By flashlight that night, Libby spread the sheet of paper out on her dresser to dry and prayed again, asking God to protect the lost man and comfort his family, but also to take care of Nick and bring him safely home.

The note was succinct, and there was no mention of his feelings, but Libby touched it with her fingertips and drew security from it, a love letter that didn't speak of love. She gained courage from looking at the firm, bold letters he had written. Nick summoned up the strength for acts of valor every day.

School was canceled again on Thursday, though the power was restored in most of Waterville that morning. It came back on after the time when school usually opened, and too many of the students' families and staff were still without electricity. The lost days would have to be paid back from planned snow days or added to the end of the school year.

At the old farmhouse, there was still no power. Libby and Kim were on the far edge of the small city. They knew crews were working on fixing the problem. They opened their refrigerator and prepared a lunch of leftovers that didn't go together but needed to be eaten or thrown away. Green beans, corn, spaghetti, a few hotdogs, milk, and melting gelatin.

They used as much as they could of what would spoil otherwise. They left the freezer closed tight, hoping the power would be restored soon. If not, they would have to deal with the bread, meat, vegetables, and fruit inside.

Libby's battery-powered radio told them that the lost hunter was still missing, and she knew Nick was still up there. The rain had stopped, but the searchers would be hiking through thick woods and underbrush. Even with rain gear, the drenching moisture would permeate their clothing, their supplies, and their skin.

Late in the afternoon, her phone rang. Libby reached for it from within a wrapped blanket. The sun had struggled out, and they had decided not to build the fire up again until dusk to conserve their shrinking woodpile in the cellar.

"Elizabeth!"

"Nick." She laughed, overjoyed to hear his voice strong

and vibrant.

"How are you girls doing?"

"All right. No power yet. We're learning to run the woodstove."

"Stay warm."

"We will. How about you?"

"I'm still in Madison. They're putting us up in a motel in Skowhegan tonight. I could drive home, but we're going out again at dawn. If he's alive, he's got to be in bad shape after last night. It was wet and cold."

"Should be warmer tonight," Libby said.

"Yes. I hope I'll be back tomorrow."

"Just keep me posted."

"I will. We have a date," he reminded her.

"I haven't forgotten. Where are we going?"

"Well, I had some things planned, but this storm might put a cramp in the

agenda. We'll have to see what's up and running tomorrow night, okay?"

"All right." Libby was silent for a moment, not wanting the conversation to end. It was so good to hear him, to know his thoughts were on her. "We prayed for you all last night at prayer meeting. Do you think that man is alive?"

"I don't know. It's a pretty big area. They found his truck yesterday."

"Was it near the river?"

"About a mile from it. Still ... unless he found cover someplace ... well, I don't know. Could be he had a heart attack, or a gun accident, or anything. But I've heard about people being lost for days and then walking out all right."

"Nick, I miss you," Libby blurted, then stood still, embarrassed, wishing she had held it back.

He said slowly, "Now, that is a really wonderful thing to hear."

She breathed then.

"I'm smiling," he said.

"Me, too."

"I miss you, too. I'll be there tomorrow if I possibly can."

"All right. I'll understand if you can't."

"No word from the Black Knight, I hope?"

"I think he's left the field," Libby said.

Chapter 29

Edge of the Map

The pulp truck rattled by at five o'clock, and Libby opened one eye. It was light, but too soon. She opened the other eye. Her bedside lamp was on, the too-bright glow streaming out above and below the ecru shade.

She jumped out of bed. It was warm in her bedroom, and she knew the oil furnace had been running for some time. She tiptoed rapidly to the bathroom and tried the faucet in the sink. Water! Wonderful, blessed water! She hurried back to her room for her clean clothes and prepared to take a shower.

The pastor called at six. They would hold school with whatever teachers and students could come. She woke Kim and Stacy, and they had their turns in the shower.

About a third of the student body was absent, and the two teachers who lived the farthest away and were still without power. Their students were absorbed into other classes for the day.

Libby was eager to teach again. The enforced break had given her time to enhance the twins unit, and she decided to begin that day, eagerly explaining to the children the projects and activities she had planned.

At three thirty, Kim drove into their driveway, and the black Fish and Wildlife Department Explorer was parked before the carport. Nick was sitting on the steps.

He stood and came toward them, smiling, as Kim brought

the Saturn to a halt. He was in his uniform, and had his heavy jacket over it, unzipped.

He opened Libby's door, and she got out. Nick's eyes sparkled, and his jaw was rough with three days' worth of whiskers. He put one hand on her arm. "I was hoping you'd be here soon. I haven't been home yet. Couldn't wait to see you."

Kim smiled at him and bustled Stacy into the house.

"Come on in," Libby said softly.

"I should go home and change and have a bath."

"Did you find him?"

He nodded gravely. "This noon. Tom almost tripped over him. He must have had a heart attack or something. No blood. They're doing an autopsy in Augusta."

Libby shook her head. "I'm sorry."

"Mm. It's too bad. We found him in an area we'd been over three or four times, but he'd tumbled right into a thicket."

The wind came, not willing to give up, and tossed Libby's long chestnut hair. She shivered and pulled her jacket closer around her. "Come in," she said again.

"Why don't I touch base at home and come back for you in an hour?"

"All right." It made sense, but she hated to have him leave so soon.

"I'll be back." He lifted his hand toward her cheek, then let it fall. "Guess my hands are cold." He smiled. "It's really good to see you."

***

He came back scrubbed and outfitted in his corduroy sport coat and clean brown pants, a blue shirt and a blue tie with thin beige and brown stripes slicing it. His hair was still damp, and he had shaved close.

"Thought maybe you were growing a beard," Kim said when she admitted him to the kitchen.

"No, just got separated from my razor for a couple of

days."

Libby was relieved to see him dressed up somewhat. She had chosen a skirt, blouse, and knit vest, but had wondered if it would be appropriate for their evening's activities.

"Aunt Libby, you look pretty," Stacy cried.

Libby scooped her up in a hug. "Thank you, baby." She smiled over Stacy's head. "Hello, Nick."

"You look great." He held out a small bunch of violets.

She gasped. "Where did you ever get those at the end of October?"

He shrugged, smiling.

She held them to her face then smiled at him. "What are we doing?"

"Well, I made a few calls to check on things, and the first stop is Colby College. There's a flute recital at five o'clock. Then we're going to have dinner at the Fieldcrest, which is back in business today, and I thought we'd end up at..." he paused, suddenly looking uncertain.

Libby's eyes widened in question.

"My parents'?" he asked.

"Let's go."

On the way, Nick recounted his adventure in sharing a hotel room with Tom Hatfield. They had hung their soaked clothing from the shower rod and on chairs near the radiator, trying vainly to dry everything before morning. Tom had snored resoundingly, and Nick had gotten up twice in the night to go to the other bed and prod him until he rolled over. In the morning, Tom had vehemently denied that he ever snored.

The recital was in progress when they located the small auditorium. They slipped in quietly and took seats toward the rear of the room, which was only half filled. Libby closed her eyes and listened to the flute and accompanying piano, trying to calm her thoughts.

She felt Nick's hand on hers and opened her eyes. He was looking at her, not the performers. She smiled, and he squeezed her hand and turned toward the stage. At the end of each selection, they applauded with the other listeners, but Nick always reclaimed her hand.

When the music had faded, he guided her back outside, down a long flight of concrete steps to the parking lot and his truck and drove to the restaurant. It was one of Waterville's plushest, but they passed the entrance to a noisy, smoky bar when they entered. Off-track betting was in full swing, and Nick glanced apprehensively toward the clamor.

The hostess ushered them into the dining room, and suddenly everything was quiet and dim, and Libby was relieved. On their table, a candle flickered in a glass holder. She sat across from Nick perusing the menu and looked up to find him studying her face.

"It's so dark in here," she murmured.

"That's the ambiance," he said solemnly. "You ready to order?"

"I think I'll have scallops if that's okay."

"Anything you want."

"Have you ever eaten here before?" Libby asked.

"Once, about ten years ago. They're known for their popovers."

The waitress placed a basket of the famous popovers on the table and filled their water glasses. She took the order and disappeared in the twilight. Nick grasped Libby's hand and quietly asked the blessing.

"So, tomorrow's the big day," Libby said.

"Yeah, opening day is always kind of crazy. Every Saturday during deer season is, really. And the day after Thanksgiving is always big too."

Libby nodded and broke open a popover. "Am I supposed to put butter on this?"

Nick ate two, slathered in butter. Libby had to admit they lived up to their reputation.

When their entrees had arrived, Nick eyed her soberly. "I really need to discuss something with you, and maybe this is as good a time as any."

Libby looked up at him, wondering what made him so serious.

"I'll be taking a test in December," he said. "There's a supervisor's opening coming up."

"Really? That's quite a promotion, isn't it?"

"Yeah, well, I'd probably get sent away to the willywacks if I got it. See, the supervisor in southern Kennebec County is retiring, and they've got to replace him. But whoever they hire or promote won't get that job. They'll transfer another supervisor with experience because it's a high-population area. The new guy will probably be sent up to western Aroostook County, where there's hardly any people. You have about four times as much territory to cover, and half the men."

"That's how they break in their supervisors?" Libby asked.

"Guess so. Everybody likes it up there in the wilderness, but nobody wants to stay there forever."

"You would." He would be in his element, she knew. Woods and water and sky, to the edge of the map and beyond.

He smiled. "I might. If it weren't so far from everybody I love."

"How far?" she asked, skipping over the chance to inquire about all the people he loved. She knew there were plenty who loved Nick, and his love for them was treasured. She didn't need to ask if she was one of them.

"Maybe a hundred and fifty or two hundred miles from here."

"Wow."

"Yeah. But there's no guarantee I would get it. They've got about ten people taking the test."

"And the high scorer gets the promotion?"

"Not necessarily. But it would have to be one of the top three, my supervisor says."

"He's encouraging you to do this, though?" Libby's brow furrowed.

"Yeah, he thinks I have a good chance. I don't know. Most of the men that are trying for it are older than me."

"I hope you get it." Pride welled up in her, and she realized she felt a certain share in Nick's prospects. As much as she had told herself she wouldn't rush into a new relationship, the bond was there, and tightening every day.

"You really want me to get it?" he asked.

"Well, yes and no."

Nick nodded. "That's sort of how I feel. I've been thinking I'd like to be the one supervising, not the one being watched, and I'd really like to spend some time in the north woods. But it's turning out to be sort of poor timing for me. Maybe I should wait."

"When will another opportunity like this come up?" Libby asked.

He shrugged. "Maybe next year, maybe not for five or ten years. You never know. It's the first time I've felt I had enough seniority and backing to try for it."

"You've got to try," Libby said with decision. "Everyone will pray for you. If God doesn't want you up there, you won't get it, if you're truly asking for His will."

He smiled. "I should have known you'd feel that way. It would be hard to go just now, though. I'm wondering if it's worth it, now that I've met you."

Chapter 30

By the Fireside

They left the topic behind, but Libby thought about it a lot. When they had finished eating and were down to coffee, because they were too full for dessert, she said, "Nick, if you got this promotion, how long would you be up north?"

"David Hersom, the guy who's up there now, has been there five years. He likes it, but my supervisor says he told him he's ready to move back to civilization, and the department will probably transfer him. He's paid his dues."

"So what does this mean?" she asked uncertainly.

"To us, you mean?"

She nodded, self-consciously.

"We'd have to sort that out, I guess."

He paid the check, and they went out to the truck in the parking lot. Nick drove down to the intersection where College Avenue met Main Street.

"There's one more thing I'd like to show you before we go out to the house." He drove down the one-way street past clothing stores, a sandwich shop, and a stationery store, and around a corner onto Front Street, which ran back the other way beside the river. He passed the newspaper office and turned in at a parking lot on the riverside, choosing a space near the corner of the lot.

"Where are we?" Libby asked.

"At the Two-Cent Bridge."

"What's that?"

"It's an old footbridge across the Kennebec. You used to have to pay a toll of two cents. Not anymore. They restored back awhile. Come on."

They got out of the truck and walked down a path toward the bridge. As they stepped out onto the span, she heard the swirl of the water below.

Nick pulled her by the hand until they were in the middle of the bridge, then he stopped.

"I like to come out here at night," he said. "It's so quiet. Not many people come down here in the winter. After the river freezes, it's really something. Like being on the moon." He leaned on the railing and looked upstream. Libby leaned beside him, looking from the left bank and the lights of downtown Waterville to the right, where the empty old Scott Paper mill loomed large and silent on the Winslow side.

"We're not far above the dam," Nick said, turning to the other side and looking downstream. "Can you hear it? The river's high now, with all this rain we've had."

They stood there without speaking. Libby couldn't see the movement of the gray water below, but she could hear it rushing over the dam. The girders of a railroad bridge rose before them, and beyond the dam was the Waterville-Winslow bridge, with cars passing steadily over it. The red taillights gleamed cheerfully in the darkness.

"When is the test?" she asked.

"December sixth. The man in Windsor is retiring at the end of the year."

"So you'd have to leave in January?"

"I'm not sure." He put his arm around her. "Like I said, I'm wondering now if I should take it."

"You could always say no, couldn't you? I mean, if you did well, and then changed your mind and didn't want it?"

"I'd hate to do that." They stood another minute. "Come on, it's cold." He took

her hand, and they walked slowly back to the truck.

"Now, you're not going to be nervous about going to my folks', are you?" he asked. "They're really looking forward to this."

"I think I'm okay." Libby took gloves off and stuffed them in her pockets. "I've seen them at church, but I don't know as I've ever actually met them."

"They're just regular folks."

He drove the familiar roads to his home.

"This is the only place you've ever lived, isn't it?" Libby asked.

"Except for college," he agreed.

"Won't you miss it?"

"Sure, if I go. But the Bible says a man's supposed to leave his father and mother at some point, and I figure that time is coming, one way or another."

"Don't they depend on you?"

"They're not old. It's not like they can't take care of themselves."

"Of course." She took a deep breath as he turned in at the driveway.

Nick's father opened the door to them and welcomed them heartily. He led them in through the woodshed that served as an entry, into the kitchen where his wife stood smiling.

"Mom, Dad, this is Elizabeth," Nick said with a touch of shy pride.

Justin Palmer put out his hand to Libby. "Pleased to meet you. Very pleased." He smiled broadly. Libby couldn't help smiling back. He was balding, and his face was merry. Chocolate brown eyes like Nick's sparkled at her from behind his glasses.

Dorothy Palmer held out her arms and embraced Libby. "Welcome, dear. Let me take your coat." Her hair was lighter than her sons', and her gray-blue eyes shone. She was sturdy of frame, and her smile was ready and genuine.

They moved into the living room where a wood fire blazed high in the brick fireplace. Libby looked around appreciatively at the comfortable furnishings. Cushions and books were prominent.

"Do you heat the whole house with wood?" she asked.

"Oh, no, not anymore," Justin said. "We put in an oil furnace about eight years ago, but we still like a wood fire when it's chilly."

"It's cozy," Libby agreed. She and Nick sat on the couch, facing the fire. His parents took rocking chairs on either side. She was soon answering their questions about school and her family and how she and Kim had managed through the blackout.

She learned that Nick's father was a supervisor for the state's Department of Transportation and had his office in Fairfield, just beyond Waterville.

"I'm mostly at my desk now," he said. "I used to be out there paving and driving a grader or a snowplow in the old days."

"I guess you're a sight more comfortable than you used to be, along about February," Dorothy said.

They talked on for an hour, and Dorothy brought a photo album to show Libby pictures of Nick's brothers and sisters and their families. "Amber's down in New Hampshire," she said, pointing to a photo of a dark-haired young woman with a slender, serious-eyed man beside her and two toddlers on their knees. "Peggy lives in Connecticut. This is her and her husband, Dan, and their son, Billy. We'll have them all here at Christmas."

"You'll have a full house," Libby said.

"Yes, six grandchildren now, counting Mike's." Dorothy turned to a photo of a serious-eyed young man in a naval dress uniform. His hair was light brown and wavy, like Dorothy's, and he had her blue-gray eyes. "Stephen is in the Navy. He's based in Norfolk, Virginia, now. I don't know if he'll get leave at Christmas or not. I hope so."

"Show her the one of all the kids," Justin said.

"Oh, well, the last time we had them all together was last

Christmas," Dorothy said. She turned back in the album to a photo of Mike, Stephen, and Nick with their sisters, seated before a Christmas tree.

"It's a nice family," Libby said.

"Now, I should show you the one of them all sitting on top of Cadillac Mountain," said Dorothy.

"Oh, Mom, that was twenty years ago," Nick said. "If you start getting out the baby pictures, I'm leaving."

She smiled and said, "Maybe another time."

Libby smiled at her. Dorothy was easy to talk to and had a merriness about her that suggested the family had lots of fun in that house.

Nick settled back on the couch and reached for her hand. Libby felt a flush creeping up her neck to her face, but she didn't remove her hand. Justin and Dorothy smiled benevolently on them and served tea and cookies. Tales of the grandchildren began to fly.

"We'd better get going," Nick said at nine thirty. "I'll be back later. Don't wait up."

"Do we ever?" Dorothy asked.

"You come back soon," Justin said to Libby, handing over her warm blue jacket.

"I'd like that. Thank you for having me."

Dorothy leaned close. "Thank you for making Nick so happy," she whispered, kissing Libby's cheek. Libby smiled at her in spite of her embarrassment and went out with Nick, through the woodshed and into the frosty night.

Stars glittered overhead. Libby stopped in the driveway to look up at them. They were so bright and close, she thought she could pick a few. Nick halted beside her, following her upward gaze, and his arm slid around her.

"I'll take you home," he said softly.

Chapter 31

Crazy Over You

Libby wished the evening wouldn't end, but she knew Nick would be up before daylight and out on his duties. She got into the truck and sat contentedly beside him the few miles to her house. The living room light was on, and a dimmer one in the kitchen.

"Looks like Kim's still up," she said. "Would you like to come in for a minute?"

He walked with her into the carport and up the steps. The door was locked, and she fumbled for her key ring, but Kim opened the door before she had the key in her hand.

"Hi, come on in," Kim said brightly. "I'm correcting math tests."

"Need any help?" Libby asked as she and Nick stepped into the kitchen.

"No, I've only got three to go, but I want to finish up before I lose my momentum. You guys will excuse me, won't you?"

"Sure," said Libby, and Nick nodded.

"There's ice cream," Kim said over her shoulder as she went into the dining room, behind the kitchen. Libby could see her papers, grade book, and calculator spread out on the dining room table.

"Want some?" asked Libby.

"Not really," Nick replied.

"I don't think I'll eat again for about three days," Libby laughed. She sobered and asked tentatively, "Take your coat off?"

He unzipped it and shrugged out of it, hanging it over the back of a kitchen chair. Libby took hers off and walked through to the living room, where the stairs went up, and laid her jacket on the railing. When she turned around, Nick was right behind her, and she jumped a little.

"Sorry."

"It's okay," she said.

He reached out to her and slowly pulled her toward him. She met his eyes gravely.

"Elizabeth."

She let him fold her against the front of his shirt, with her cheek against the lapel of the warm corduroy jacket. "So, our first date is over, and we lived," she said.

"Not quite over." He held her close, and his cheek came down gently on her hair. "Are you getting used to me?"

"It's easier than I thought," she whispered.

He kissed her then, with his right arm around her waist and his left hand lost in her thick hair. Her hands crept slowly around him, and when he released her, she collapsed against his shoulder.

"Could we pray?" he asked. "About my job, I mean, and— well, everything."

She nodded and led him to the couch. He held her hand firmly and closed his eyes. His prayer was simple and direct, giving thanks to God for the chance to advance in his profession, and asking for God's perfect will. Then he thanked God for Libby, and a flash of tenderness and gratitude went through her. When Nick had finished, she prayed quietly, giving thanks for the situation God had put her in and the joy she was finding there.

When she opened her eyes, he put his hand up to her hair, brushing it back from her cheek. "Elizabeth, I love you."

She tried to keep her breathing even.

"I don't want to rush things," he said, "but I know it's true. I may not see you for a while, and I want you to hear it in person. I love you. I've never felt so certain about anything before."

She smiled, unable for a moment to say anything.

"Do you think you could … love me?" he asked. "Maybe not right away, but later? I don't think I'd want to go up north for five years alone anymore." He laughed a little. "On the other hand, I don't think I'd want to stay here for five years alone, either. Libby—Elizabeth, could you?"

"I could," she whispered. "I do love you." She swallowed hard. He slid his arms around her again and kissed her tenderly.

"I'd better go," he said, but he didn't move.

They heard Kim pushing back her chair in the dining room and putting away her things.

Nick sighed. "I'll try to come by tomorrow if I can."

"You don't have to. It's your busiest day of the year."

"Just about. But I want to see you if I can."

He stood up, and Libby stood with him. Kim appeared in the kitchen doorway. "Forgot to tell you your mother called," she said to Libby.

"Oh, it's late now. I'll call her tomorrow," Libby said.

"Well, she said you could call her up until eleven."

Libby glanced at her watch. It was quarter past ten.

"I'll get going, and you can call her," Nick said.

"Good night, Nick," Kim said. "I'm going up and check Stacy." She headed up the stairs.

Libby and Nick went into the kitchen, and he picked up his jacket. He turned toward her and held out his arms. She melted into them and slid her right arm up around his neck.

"I love you," he said again. "I'm absolutely crazy over you, but it's more than that. I think God might have a future for us."

Libby couldn't respond to that. He kissed her again, then stood looking down at her with soft eyes for a moment. His lips brushed her forehead, then he pulled on his jacket and went out. Libby waved and closed the door quietly.

"Mom, it's me," she said when her mother answered the telephone in Westbrook. "Sorry to be so late."

"It's all right," Sandra Sharpe said. "Your roommate said you had a date tonight."

"Yes. My first date ... since Aiden."

"You'd heard from Aiden last week. You said he called while you were out. Did he call back?"

"Yes, he called first, and then he came up here."

"He did?" Sandra was startled. "Did he fly?"

"As far as Boston. He was there for something else, some education conference, I think. He rented a car and drove up Sunday."

"Did you two talk things out?"

"I don't think so, not really. I didn't want to talk to him. He was ... overbearing."

"Really? I always thought he was so polite."

"He seemed to think he could just walk back into my life and pick things up where he'd trampled them in the mud and make everything fine again."

"So you sent him packing?"

"Yes," said Libby. "I'm done with him, Mom."

"All right, dear. I can understand that, I guess. But you had a date tonight."

"Yes."

"Do you want to tell me about it?"

She drew a deep breath. "Mom, he's great. You'd like him. I know you would. I—I met his parents tonight, and they're wonderful people."

"He's a Christian?" her mother asked.

"Of course."

"Just checking."

"Mom, I love him."

"Libby, are you sure?"

"Yes. I know it seems sudden, but it's not, really. This was our first real date, but he's been around for a while, and I was kind of holding him off, but now—well, now I don't want to put him off anymore."

"That sounds serious."

"I think it might be."

"Bring him down for Thanksgiving," Sandra said.

"I don't know if that's possible. He has a lot of family here, and he has to work, maybe Thanksgiving Day, and certainly the day after. And that Saturday is the last day of hunting season. I just don't know, Mom."

"What does hunting season have to do with it?" her mother asked in exasperation.

"Didn't I say? Sorry. He's a game warden. He has to be out there during hunting season, which is all of November. Well, except Sundays."

"So bring him down on a Sunday."

"Maybe … maybe I could. I'll ask him."

Chapter 32

Run Quick

Libby ignored the pulp truck in the morning, but by six thirty she was hearing gunshots – some distant poofs and others sharp cracks at closer range.

She got up and dressed in corduroy slacks and a sweatshirt. Kim and Stacy slept late, and Libby had her devotions and did some paperwork for school. She planned to go shopping that afternoon, and she started working on a grocery list.

Her phone rang, and she leaped to get it before the noise could waken the sleepers.

"Elizabeth, it's me."

She smiled. "Hello, Nick."

"I'll run by there about eleven o'clock, I think."

"Great. Can you take your lunch hour here?"

"Maybe. How about we say eleven thirty, then?"

"Fine. How's it going?"

"There are a lot of hunters out this morning."

"Any of them successful?"

"Yeah, I've seen three or four tagged deer already. I think Tom and I will head over Unity way after lunch, but I'm spending the morning in this area."

"I called my mother," Libby said.

"Everything okay?"

"Yes, she was just concerned about me. I'd called her last

week about Aiden, and I was a little bit upset then."

"All is calm now?"

"Yes, I haven't been this tranquil in months." She hesitated, then said what was on her heart. "It's you, Nick. You've made the change in my attitude. You and God. You're inseparably linked in it. And Nick?"

"What?"

"My parents would like to meet you."

"Are they coming up?"

"No, I was hoping sometime you might—" she stumbled to a stop. "Maybe sometime on a Sunday we could go down? I mean, if that's not too much—"

"I'd like that. It would have to be a Sunday, though, unless you want to wait another month."

"No, anytime."

"Well, how about tomorrow?"

"Really? Just like that?"

"Well, sure. I mean, if it's okay with them. You've met my folks and seen my native habitat. I'd like to see yours."

"I'll call my mom again," said Libby.

"I've got to get moving. I'm sorry."

"It's okay."

"Look for me around half past eleven."

Libby decided to go to the grocery store right away. She left Kim a note and headed out, shopping list in hand.

When she returned, Kim and Stacy were eating a belated breakfast.

"Hey! What does this cryptic note mean?" Kim asked. "Nick is coming for lunch?"

"Uh-huh."

"Today?"

"Yes, if he can. That's why I went shopping so early. I hope you didn't have an urgent need for anything that wasn't on the list."

Libby made another trip to her car, and when she returned Kim was putting away the groceries.

"So, what are we feeding him?" Kim asked.

"I thought pork chops. They were on sale."

"Great. What else?"

"Mashed potatoes and applesauce and tossed salad?"

"Good. What do you want me to do?"

"Nothing," said Libby. "I'll do it. Just enjoy your daughter today."

"We'll make dessert," Kim decided.

Libby sat down with a bag of potatoes and a paring knife. Stacy helped her mother get out the ingredients for a cake and measure them carefully into a bowl, then mix them.

When the pan was in the oven, Kim said, "Now what do you want to do, Stacy?"

"Swing."

"Oh, honey, I don't know. Hunting season's started." Kim turned to Libby. "Do you think it's safe out there?"

"I don't know," said Libby. "I heard a lot of shooting this morning. But the swing set is so close to the house…"

"All right," Kim relented, "but we have to wear the orange vests and hats. She had purchased gear for herself and Stacy, and they put it on, laughing and modeling their blaze orange fashions for Libby.

"It's pretty chilly," Libby said. "Better wear mittens."

When they were bundled up, the two went out to the back yard, charging Libby to take the cake out of the oven when it was done. She went on with her lunch preparations, setting the table, and she started cooking the meat at eleven o'clock to have it ready for Nick's early lunch hour. The timer rang, and she took Kim's cake out of the oven and set it on a cooling rack.

Glancing at the clock, she grabbed her jacket and slipped it on as she went out the door. She rounded the corner of the house and saw Kim pushing Stacy on the swing.

"Higher!" Stacy squealed. Kim's white mittens went up to meet the swing board as it flew back toward her.

"Cake's done," Libby called.

"Okay, we'd better go in," Kim said, preparing to stop the swing.

"Three more pushes, Mommy," begged Stacy.

Kim laughed. "All right, but that's it. I'm tired!"

She gave a mighty push. "One! I hear a car," she said. "Must be Nick."

Libby turned toward the driveway, but the carport obscured her view.

"Two!" Libby heard tires on gravel, and she started toward the carport.

A gunshot cracked from the woods. She turned back, saying, "That was close!"

Kim was staring at her, eyes fixed, mouth open. "Libby," she said softly.

Then she fell.

"Kim!"

Libby ran to her and was nearly brained by the swing board as Stacy continued her flight. She grabbed the chain and stopped the swing.

"Stacy, run quick and get Mr. Palmer!" Libby said, too loudly, setting Stacy on the ground. "Go now!" Wide-eyed, Stacy ran for the driveway.

She bent over her friend. "Kim?"

Kim moaned. She lay on her stomach in the brown grass, gasping.

"Kim, honey!" Fear stabbed at Libby. "Kim, can you hear me?"

"What happened?" Nick asked, appearing at the corner of the carport with Stacy. He ran toward the swing set.

"Kim's hurt." Libby's eyes were huge. "Nick, I think she's been shot."

Dismay crossed his face. He knelt and put his hand on Kim's back, where a hole perforated the orange vest. He turned Kim over gently. "Kim, can you hear me?"

Kim looked up at him, baffled. "Nick?"

"Yes, where does it hurt?"

"My back. Nick, what happened?"

"Lie still, Kim." He unzipped her jacket and opened it.

"She was pushing Stacy on the swing, and I heard a shot," said Libby.

He glanced from her face to the woods a hundred yards away. Kim moaned as he pulled her jacket sleeve off carefully and lifted her up against him. Libby gasped. Blood was oozing through the fibers of Kim's off-white sweater. Nick laid her down gently on her side and pulled a handkerchief from his pocket, pressing it to the wound.

"Go call 911," he said. Libby stood up. She looked toward the woods and saw a man in an orange vest approaching, carrying a rifle.

"Nick, look!"

Nick turned his head and stared. "Hold this," he commanded.

Libby went to her knees, put her hand on the bloody handkerchief, and pressed it firmly. Kim shivered and gasped.

Chapter 33

A Flash of White

Nick strode toward the man. The hunter eyed him warily as he approached.

"Did you fire that rifle?" Nick demanded.

"Yeah, I took a shot at a deer." He looked around nervously. "Didn't realize there was a house right here," he muttered. He was past fifty, Nick judged, with graying hair clipped short. A white-collar worker out for recreation.

Nick reached out and took the man's rifle by the leather sling.

"You'd better let me carry this."

"I don't understand."

"A woman's been shot." Nick watched his face.

The man's cheek twitched. "Shot? Don't look at me."

"Do you think you hit that deer?" Nick asked.

"Well, I hope so. Couldn't see it all."

"Come on, we can't waste time." Nick turned and walked swiftly back to the swing set, with the hunter following more slowly.

"Go make that call," Nick said to Libby, laying the rifle down and taking over her post.

Libby looked from him to Kim. Stacy was standing by the swing, staring fearfully at her mother, her red mittens in front of her mouth. Nick knelt and pressed on the wound as Libby ran quickly into the house.

"Is it bad?" The man ventured.

Nick didn't bother to look at him. "Pretty bad. Just don't you go anywhere, you hear me?"

"I—I won't, but I didn't shoot that woman."

"We'll find out," Nick said sternly. "What's your name?"

"John Austin." He came a step closer and stood beneath the crossbar of the swing set, wringing his hands. "This is really bad," he said after a minute.

"You're telling me?" Nick asked. Kim's breathing was very shallow, and he fought panic. He couldn't let her die right here with Stacy watching.

The kitchen window twenty feet away went up. Libby stuck her head out. "Nick! I'm talking to the dispatcher. What should I tell her?"

"Get the EMTs here fast!"

"They're coming."

"Just a minute." He turned to the hunter. "You get down here and put pressure on this handkerchief. Don't let go!"

Austin knelt beside him and put out his hand. His face paled and he started to turn away.

"Do it now," Nick yelled. The man slowly put his hand where Nick's was and pressed on the cloth.

Nick got up and ran to the window. "Give me the phone."

Libby passed him her cell.

"We've got a twenty-five-year-old woman with a gunshot wound to the back," he told the dispatcher. "It's an inch and a half to the left of her spine, about the level of the bottom of the lung."

"She's twenty-seven," Libby said.

Nick decided that wasn't important in this situation. To the dispatcher, he said, "There doesn't seem to be an exit wound, and we're putting pressure on the entrance wound. What else can we do?"

"Just hang on," the man said. "They'll be there soon."

Nick shook his head. There had to be more than that. "She's bleeding a lot." He looked up at Libby and held out the phone. She exchanged it for a clean dish towel. "I'm going to send Stacy in," he said. "Can you drop a blanket out the window?"

Libby nodded and told the dispatcher she was going for a blanket and set the telephone down on the counter. Nick went back to swing set and squatted down near Stacy.

"Baby, I want you to go inside with Aunt Libby."

Stacy stared at him with horror on her face. "Mommy's hurt."

Nick pulled her into his arms. "You pray, okay honey? I need to help your mommy now. You go inside." He squeezed her, then released her, facing her toward the carport. He went back to Kim and took over from Austin, wadding the dish towel against Kim's back. The hunter sat down heavily on the ground beside him, looking queasy.

"I can't have done this," he said. "It was a deer. I saw—"

"You saw what?" Nick asked grimly.

"I saw the flag."

Nick said nothing. He had heard too many stories of hunters who fired at a glimpse of white or the sound of stamping in a thicket.

"I was back in the woods a little, and the deer was running across the field. I could just see into the open a little, and I saw its tail flash," the hunter said.

Nick shook his head. Her white mittens, he thought, seeing Kim stretching upward to catch the swing board. He took her limp wrist with one hand and began counting her pulse.

Libby came around the corner with a folded quilt in her arms. "Nick, how's she doing?"

"She's unconscious, breathing is shallow, pulse about a hundred. Are they coming?"

Libby repeated his words into the phone. "They'll be there soon. The driver is on Lincoln Street."

"Go out by the road and flag them down," he yelled.

"I put Stacy on the phone with the dispatcher. Is that okay? I told the dispatcher how young she is."

"Sure."

Dear God, let them be on time.

Kim moaned softly.

Straining his ears, he thought he heard a siren in the distance. Three seconds later, he was sure. When the vehicle came even with the driveway, Libby came running around the carport.

"Nick, they're here."

"Bring them right out here. I can't let go," he said. Kim's respirations were shallow, but she was still breathing.

Libby went back around the corner and the siren stopped, but he heard another approaching. Two EMTs followed Libby at last to the swing set.

"Let me take a look, sir," a female EMT said, setting her bag down beside Kim. Her name tag said *Laura.* Her partner, Brian, knelt on Kim's other side.

Nick looked around and saw Libby leaning against one leg of the swing set, watching them work.

"How long has she been on the ground?" Laura asked.

"About ten minutes," Nick replied.

"I'll take over, sir," Brian said, placing his hands firmly on the bloody towel.

Nick stood up slowly. His hands and the front of his state-issue winter jacket were bloody.

Chapter 34

With the Family

"Aunt Libby?"

Libby and Nick turned quickly. Stacy stood behind Libby. Her chest ached at the little girl's woebegone face.

"The lady said I could hang up." Stacy held out the phone.

Libby picked her up and hugged her fiercely, turning Stacy away from where Kim lay. "I'm sorry. I should have come back in for you." She pocketed the phone.

"Is Mommy okay?"

"No, baby, she's hurt. They're going to take her to the hospital."

Nick walked around close to them and squeezed Libby's shoulder. A police officer appeared at the corner of the carport.

"Randy." Nick greeted like an old friend. They were close enough in age that Libby figured they could have been schoolmates.

"What happened here?" Randy asked. The EMTs were preparing Kim for transport.

Nick drew him a few paces away, toward the farm lane, and spoke to him in low tones. Libby turned to look swiftly, past the EMTs. John Austin still sat on the ground, incredulously watching the proceedings.

She squeezed Stacy hard. "We'll go to the hospital when the ambulance leaves and make sure they take good care of Mommy." Stacy whimpered but said nothing.

After a minute, the officer approach the hunter.

"Sir, is this your rifle?" Randy asked, nodding toward the gun that lay on the dead grass.

"Y-yes, but I didn't do this."

"We'll let the lab say for sure," Randy said. "Could you please stand up, sir? You need to come with me."

The EMTs had brought the stretcher around the house, and they lifted Kim onto it.

"Should we go to the hospital?" Libby asked Laura, the nearest EMT.

"Yes, you can go now. We'll be at the ER in about ten minutes."

Libby took Stacy into the house. She turned off the stove, placing the pan of overdone meat in the refrigerator to be dealt with later.

"Stacy, I'm just going to get my purse, then we'll go to the hospital where they're taking Mommy."

Libby ran up the stairs. When she came down, Nick was in the kitchen with Stacy, washing his hands at the sink.

"Libby!"

He grabbed a dish towel and hastily wiped his hands. She went rapidly toward him.

"Wait." He unzipped his bloody jacket and dropped it to the floor, then took her in his arms. "I'm so sorry." He held her close, then bent his knees and picked Stacy up, gathering her into his embrace too. "Let's pray for a minute, and then we'll get to the hospital."

"Your lunch hour—" Libby immediately felt foolish. Lunch hours didn't matter at a time like this.

"I'll call on the radio," he said. "I'll stay with you."

"The police will handle this?" Libby asked.

"Yes, they're sending more men. But I'm glad I was here."

"Me too." The tears came, and she sobbed against his shoulder, so very thankful for his strength and calmness, his quiet authority. She turned, groping for the tissue box, and Stacy took one too.

Nick held her and Stacy while he prayed for Kim. Libby added a fervent amen but didn't feel she could voice her petitions yet.

"Better call the pastor," he said.

Libby took out her phone once more and scrolled for the parsonage number.

"Mrs. Wilson, it's Libby Sharpe. Kim's been shot. Yes, a hunter shot her by mistake. It's very serious. Nick Palmer is here. We're going to the hospital. Yes. Thank you." She closed the connection and looked up at Nick. "They'll meet us there."

"All right, let's go."

Libby picked up her purse and locked the door.

"Come in my Explorer," Nick said.

"Shouldn't I drive? You'll have to bring us home later."

"That's okay. Come on."

He strapped Stacy into the back seat, and Libby got in with her. Nick turned his blue light on as he pulled out onto the road. When they were rolling smoothly, he called on the radio and gave the message for Tom Hatfield that he had responded to a hunting accident. The victim was a personal friend, he told the dispatcher, and he was going to the hospital.

A few minutes later, as they sped out Kennedy Drive, he received a call.

"Three-two-seven, you are cleared from duty for the rest of the day. Stay with your shooting victim and assist the police as needed."

"Ten-four." Nick drove silently to the emergency entrance of the hospital.

Libby sat with her arms around Stacy. Mark and Sarah Wilson were just arriving at the parking lot when they got there, and they entered the hospital together, with Nick carrying Stacy.

The pastor went to the desk to talk to the charge nurse.

"Libby and I can go in and see her for a minute, before they take her to surgery," he reported.

Libby followed Mark into the trauma area, and she went

181

close to the gurney where Kim lay on her stomach.

"Kim." There was no response, and her eyes remained closed. Kim's back rose and fell rapidly as she breathed.

Libby's heart wrenched. Kim seemed so fragile, as though she might stop breathing at any time. She turned hopelessly to the pastor.

"Is there anything we can do?" Mark Wilson asked the doctor.

"Just stay with the family, and we'll do what we can for her," the doctor replied.

They went back into the waiting room. Nick sat on a chair holding Stacy on his lap. The little girl leaned back against his shoulder, her face a mask of grief. Sarah Wilson sat next to Nick but rose when her husband and Libby and appeared.

"She's unconscious," Pastor Wilson said. "We can go upstairs to another waiting room near the operating room. I'll call the prayer chain leaders from up there." He turned to Libby. "What about Kim's family?"

"Her parents," Libby cried. "We need to call them. They live in Massachusetts."

"Do you have a number?"

"No, but I'm sure I could find it at home. Kim's address book is in her bedroom."

"I'll go for it," Nick said.

"No," the pastor said. "I'll go."

"It's all right," Nick told him. "They might need you here." He stood and said to Stacy, "You stay with Aunt Libby, pumpkin."

Libby handed him the house key and explained how to find the address book.

"Should I just call her parents when I get the number?" he asked.

"Yes, thank you. That would save them time."

He left, and Libby felt doubly bereft. She and Stacy went with the Wilsons to the upper waiting room. The pastor called several people in the church, and half an hour later Jill and

Mike Palmer arrived. Jill opened her arms to Libby, and Libby cried then.

"Where are the kids?" Libby asked.

"They're with the Mitchells," Jill said. "Is Kim's family coming?"

"Nick went to the house to get the phone number and call them."

"Nick was here?"

Libby sniffed and nodded. "He was at the house when it happened. Just coming by for lunch. Jill, I don't know what I'd have done if he hadn't been there. There was this man coming out of the woods with his rifle. Nick made him stay and help. It was awful." She cried some more, but by the time Nick returned she had regained control.

"Nicky!" Mike stood up and went to his brother when Nick came through the waiting room door.

"Hey, Mike. Thanks for being here." Nick gripped his brother's hand. "I tried to call you, but I guess someone else did."

"Pastor Mark did. Are Kim's parents coming?"

"Yes, they should be here in about four hours." He tossed his blood-stained coat on a chair and went straight to Libby. Her eyelids were red and puffy, but she was no longer crying. She smiled tremulously as he approached her. He sank down beside her, putting his arm around her shoulders, and no one seemed to think it odd.

"How we doing?" he asked softly.

"We're holding on and praying," Libby said.

He squeezed her a little. "Her folks are leaving right away. They'll stay as long as she needs them."

"Maybe I should take Stacy home with me," Sarah suggested. "The poor little thing is white as a sheet."

"Let's see if we can get a progress report," the pastor said. He left the room and came back a few minutes later.

"The bullet hit the bottom of her lung, and it's partially collapsed. One rib is broken. There's some damage to the liver.

But they think she'll recover in time, praise God."

Nick drew Stacy close to him and looked the little girl in the eyes. "Did you hear that, pumpkin? Mommy's going to be all right. She'll have to stay here and rest for a few days, and she'll probably have to rest for a while when she goes home, but she'll get better."

Stacy's lips quivered, and she gave him a tremulous smile. She dove into Nick's lap then, and he held her tight, rubbing her back.

"Let's give thanks," Mark said.

They prayed together, and Libby put Stacy's jacket on her.

"I'll keep her with me and feed her supper," Sarah told Libby. "Call me when you're ready to go home, and I'll meet you."

"We'll bring Pastor Mark home later and pick up Stacy," Nick offered.

Chapter 35

The Most Awful Thing

Throughout the afternoon, they sat in the waiting room. Nick took Libby out in the hall to walk for a few minutes, and they stopped to look out a window at the end of the hallway, over the vast parking lot below. He put his arm around her, and she leaned on his shoulder.

"We need to thank God for this." He'd been thinking about it for some time, but he wasn't sure how Libby would react.

"I can thank God that she'll make it, but for the shooting? It doesn't make sense."

"Not to us," he agreed.

"You can actually thank God that this happened?"

"He knows what He's doing," Nick said quietly.

She sighed heavily.

Slowly he said, "We may never know why God allowed this to happen, but we know it's part of His plan."

After a long moment, Libby said, "I guess you're right, but it's hard, Nick."

"Yes." He turned toward her and put both arms around her, holding her head tight against the shoulder of his green uniform shirt. "I hate to think how I'd be feeling if that were you in there right now."

"Could you still thank God?"

"I think … I'd have to. But He would have to give me a lot of courage."

"He would," said Libby with wonder. "I've never known anyone like you before. People say we're supposed to give thanks in all things, but I never before knew anyone who could actually put it into practice."

He stroked her hair. "I love you, Elizabeth. And I know God loves me even more. If He cares that much about me, He won't allow things to happen to me without a purpose."

Libby closed her eyes. Nick stood holding her by the window for a long time. At last she straightened.

"We have so much to be thankful for."

"Yes." Nick felt a surge of gratitude for Libby herself, and for her ability to accept the day's events.

"Let's go back to the waiting room," she said.

They walked slowly back down the hallway and joined the others.

The doctor came in just after four o'clock.

"Mrs. Richardson is in the recovery room. She'll stay in the hospital at least a week, but she should mend."

"Her parents haven't arrived yet," Pastor Wilson said.

"Well, she won't be awake for some time. If you tell the nurses when they get here, they can take her parents to her."

Kim's parents, Paul and Virginia Rutledge, arrived an hour later, and the pastor talked and prayed with them. Libby invited them to stay at the house in Kim's room that night. A nurse came and took them to the recovery room to sit with their daughter.

At last Nick took the pastor and Libby in his Explorer to the parsonage, where they left Pastor Mark and bundled Stacy into the Explorer. Back at the farmhouse, Nick called his parents, updated them on Kim, and told them he wouldn't be home until late.

"I'll stay until the Rutledges get here," he told Libby.

"You don't have to."

"I know." Nothing was going to make him leave now. Libby seemed to grasp that.

"Thank you. I'll go up and change Kim's bed for them, I

guess."

"What ever happened to lunch?" Nick asked.

She smiled a little. "I put the meat in the fridge. The rest is probably inedible. You can do some scouting if you want."

She was gone twenty minutes, preparing the bedroom. Nick enlisted Stacy, and when Libby returned he was carefully watching two pans on the stove and saying to Stacy, "That's right, your Grampy and Grammy are going to sleep here tonight." Stacy was carefully lining up forks and plates on the table. The three sat down to slightly leathery pork chops, green beans, applesauce, and cake without frosting.

***

Libby allowed Stacy to watch a cartoon tape after supper, hoping it would distract her from her mother's injury. She held the little girl on her lap, and Nick sat beside them on the couch.

"Did you ever call your folks?" he asked softly.

"No, too many things happened. We should probably stay here tomorrow, don't you think?"

"Probably. Maybe we'll go down next week, then?"

"Yes. We'll see how Kim is in a couple of days, and if she's doing well I'll arrange it."

When the tape ended, Libby sent Stacy upstairs to put on her pajamas and brush her teeth.

"Nick, I'd have collapsed if you hadn't been here. Kim— that man—" she shuddered. "It's the most awful thing I ever lived through." The confrontation with Aiden Knight seemed trivial in comparison.

He nodded solemnly.

"I'm ready, Aunt Libby," Stacy called plaintively from the head of the stairs.

"I'll go tuck her in." Libby went up the stairs and took Stacy into her bedroom.

"When will Mommy come home?" the little girl asked. Her puffy eyes swam with tears.

"Not for a few days, honey. We've got to let her stay there and rest and let the doctors help her get better. But she will come home. And your Grandpa and Grammy will be here when you wake up in the morning."

"Promise?"

"Yes, I promise."

Libby prayed and listened as Stacy lifted her voice, eyes shut tight.

"Dear God, *please* make Mommy better soon!"

Chapter 36

Are You Saying Yes?

When Libby went back downstairs, Nick was signing off on a phone call.

"I called the hospital. She's awake, and her folks are with her. They may be late getting out here, but they'll come."

"You don't have to stay, Nick."

He said slowly, "I'd like to, unless you don't want me to. I mean, now that our chaperon has gone to bed … maybe I'd better leave."

"Come here." Libby put her arms around him, and he held on to her. "You've done so much for us today! I can't tell you how much it's meant to me to have you here."

"Libby, I love you. I want to be here for you always." He sounded almost apologetic. "I don't mean to pressure you, but I've got to tell you how I feel."

"Nick, Nick." She clung to him. "I love you too. You're not pressuring me."

He leaned back a little, so he could see her face. "Can I just tell you something? And you won't get upset?"

"Anything," she said.

"I've asked God, if it's His will, to let me have you as my wife."

Slowly she lowered her head, resting against his arm.

"Are you upset?" he asked.

"I promised I wouldn't be."

"If you hadn't promised, would you be?"

"I don't think so."

His arms tightened around her.

"Libby, marry me. Please. I know we've only had one official date, but that whole business is irrelevant. I know you well enough now, and I think you know me pretty well."

She bit her lip. She had said yes once before and regretted it. She didn't want to mistake the security Nick made her feel for lasting love.

"You're not saying anything," he observed.

"I'm scared out of my wits."

"I'll do it the old-fashioned way." He dropped to one knee and held her hand, looking up into her eyes. "Elizabeth Sharpe, will you marry me?"

She laughed a little laugh and tousled his hair gently. "Now, that is *really* scary. The last time I answered that question, it caused me a lot of heartache."

Nick winced and got to his feet. "I can't promise you'll never have heartache again, but I vow I'll never cause it deliberately. Whatever your heartaches are, I'll be there with you to share them. I'll never leave you, Libby. I'll never reject you or walk away from you angry."

"Those are pretty big promises, Nick."

"I know."

"What if I did something awful that made you terribly angry?"

"We'd talk about it and work it out somehow, with God's help. But you wouldn't."

She smiled. "How do you know? You say we know each other, but we don't, really. Not well. We've only known each other a few weeks."

"It's enough. I know you love God, and you're committed to follow Christ. That's all I ask. Follow Christ, and follow me."

"To Aroostook County?"

"Aha."

"Aha, what?"

"Is that a sticking point? Because I'll call my supervisor right now and tell him I don't want to take the test."

"Actually, I've been thinking it might be rather fun to spend a few years in the north woods with you."

He turned her face toward him and looked deep into her eyes, then bent down and kissed her lips gently.

"I'd be entirely dependent on you," she said. "I'm totally helpless in the woods."

"I'll teach you. You're a quick study." His voice cracked a little. "I'll buy you books on survival and take you shooting until you're a crack shot. I'll make you fire a thousand rounds a week until you're unbeatable."

"So if any beer cans attack us, I can hold them off until you get there?" she asked with a laugh.

"I might not get the position," he said.

"Then we'd stay here."

"Yes." He locked her gaze again. "Elizabeth, are you saying yes? Are you telling me you will ... or are you just having fun with me?"

"I wouldn't do that, Nick." She eyed him thoughtfully. "I guess I'm—well—I want to say yes. I'm leaning that way, at least. It just seems so fast, no matter what you say. Don't you think we should take some more time?"

"I'll come to court you and sit in your parlor every night that I'm free."

She laughed.

He scrutinized her face, and he could see that she wasn't ready to say quite what he wanted to hear. A compromise would be better than a flat-out no, he decided. "How about we give it a few more weeks, and then I'll ask you again?"

"If you still want to then," Libby said quietly.

An intense dislike for Aiden Knight rose up in him. Knight had shattered the self-esteem of this remarkable woman. Nick wished he could have known her before the Black Knight had done his work.

"Libby, I keep telling you, this isn't going away. My feelings won't change, except to get deeper. I'm not going to give you any reason for disappointment." He smiled ruefully. "Does that sound arrogant?"

"Not the way you say it."

"Good, because I don't mean it to be. If anything, I'm desperate."

"Desperate?"

"Yes. When I first saw you, I thought, no way. Not a chance. But every time I saw you, I wanted more and more for you to like me. To love me."

"When we went to Bangor?" Libby asked, her delicate eyebrows rising in disbelief.

"Now, that was torture," he admitted. "I was in agony. Couldn't seem to say anything right that night."

"Me either, so I quit trying. I thought you hated me."

"Oh, Libby!" He lifted her chin and looked into her eyes, so sad, and yet so trusting. He didn't ever want to cause her grief. "I'm going to kiss you one more time, and then I'm going to go home."

"All right. That would probably be best."

Chapter 37

End of October

Nick met Libby at the church before Sunday School started, and they took Stacy to her class then sat together on one of the white pews.

"Kim's parents went to the hospital, and I'm taking Stacy after lunch," she told him.

"How's Kim doing?"

"Resting. The doctors are optimistic." It seemed the normal thing now to sit beside Nick, waiting for the service to begin. Libby wondered why she had ever quailed at the thought of being close to him.

Justin and Dorothy Palmer came to sit with them during the worship service, and Dorothy embraced Libby.

"We've been praying for Kim and Stacy," she said, "but also for you and my son."

"Thank you, Mrs. Palmer. It's been ... a bit of a bumpy ride."

"Things are smoothing out?" Dorothy asked.

"I think so." Libby looked down at her hands. "We've both learned that it's okay to be a little nervous. That's helping us get over it, I think."

Dorothy smiled delightedly. "I've prayed so long for Nick. He's become such a fine man, but he's been very lonely."

"What are you girls whispering about?" Justin leaned forward to look past his wife at Libby.

"Not much," Dorothy told him.

"Don't worry, Dad, I have good ears," Nick said lazily, staring straight ahead.

Libby whirled around and stared at him. He gave a little shrug. "She's right. I was. I hope it's over."

Libby and Dorothy both smiled.

***

Nick took Libby and Stacy to Burger King for Stacy's favorite lunch, then drove to the hospital. They went up to Kim's room, and her parents welcomed them in the hallway, thanking Nick profusely for his part in Kim's rescue.

"Libby told us last night what you did," Mr. Rutledge said. "Kim might have bled to death if you hadn't been there and known what to do."

"That man," said Mrs. Rutledge, "the one who shot her. Is he in custody?"

"Yes, ma'am, the police took him in yesterday. He could have made bail by now, I don't know. They haven't proved yet that he did it, but the officer who arrested him, Randy LaChance, confiscated his rifle. The surgeon was supposed to turn the bullet over to the police if they recovered it. If it came from his gun, we'll know."

"How can someone shoot at a flash of white like that?" Mr. Rutledge shook his head.

"I don't know." Nick frowned. "Last year, we had a guy who shot a pickup truck, thinking it was a deer. A red pickup with the engine running. He saw movement and let off a round. Really scary."

"Do you think it could have been someone else?" Kim's mother asked.

Nick shook his head. "Not really, but you have to be careful and not rule out possibilities in a case like this. The police are asking anyone who was hunting in that area yesterday to talk to them. If it wasn't John Austin, they need to know where to start looking."

Kim opened her eyes when Libby spoke to her.

"Kim, honey, you're going to be okay. I love you. Just rest and get strong."

"Stacy," said Kim.

"Stacy's here." Libby brought Stacy close, and Kim smiled.

"Hello, baby." She looked at Libby again. "Is Nick with you?"

"Yes. Do you want to see him?"

Nick stepped over close and said, "Kim, we're praying for you."

She moved her hand slightly, and Nick bent closer.

"Thank you, Nick."

He smiled and said, "That's okay."

***

After half an hour, they took Stacy to Mike and Jill Palmer's so she could spend the afternoon playing with Rachel. Libby and Nick sat down with his brother and sister-in-law and drank coffee. After they discussed Kim's condition, the talk turned to the warden supervisor's test.

"Hey, that would be great if you could get it," Mike said. "Man, they'll give you a house if you go up there."

"Really?" Libby asked.

"Well, yeah," Nick said. "In the territory we're talking about, on the Quebec border, most of the land is owned by big paper companies. The department built a house for the supervisor, and they have housing for the men under him too. Three men, I think, or maybe four."

"So you could hoard your pay while you were up there," Jill said. "No rent."

Mike made a face. "As if he's paying rent now."

"Hey, I pay rent," Nick said.

"We'd miss you," Jill told him. She looked at Libby, who

195

sipped her coffee and said nothing.

Mike eyed his brother. "So, did you two go out Friday night? Mom said—"

"He doesn't need to know everything your mother said today," Jill cut in.

"Okay, well, I was just curious."

"Yes, we went out," said Nick.

Libby smiled.

"Met the folks?" Mike asked in her general direction.

"Yes, your parents are wonderful," Libby replied.

They left Stacy with Jill, and Nick drove back to the church. Libby drove her car home with Nick tailing her. When they got to the house, he walked out by the swing set to look at the scene of the shooting again while Libby ran inside and changed her clothes.

"Want to walk?" he asked when she came back out in wool pants and her parka. "There's no hunting today."

"All right." She fell into step beside him, and they headed for the paved road.

"Did your mother get the blood out of your other jacket?" Libby asked.

"She was soaking it last night."

The nearest neighbor was a quarter of a mile down the road. When the house came into view, Libby said, "Jill and I try to distract Stacy every time we drive by this house."

Nick looked toward the frame house and saw scarecrows and people made of stuffed clothing with pumpkin heads sitting on the porch and the lawn. In a tree near the road, one of the effigies hung from a noose. Plastic pumpkins lined the driveway, and a plastic witch stirred a caldron in the middle of the lawn. A life-size skeleton leaned against the corner of the porch.

He nodded toward the hanging dummy. "Pretty gruesome."

"It's horrible," Libby said. "I'll be so glad when Halloween is over."

"Did you buy candy for trick-or-treaters?"

"Kim said she didn't get any last year, because she's so far out from town. I did buy a few candy bars, though, just in case. They're stashed in the cupboard."

"Well, tomorrow morning those folks will have their witch down and their Santa up," Nick speculated.

"I hope so. Santa I can deal with, but not those ugly things."

"You can eat your leftover candy then." Nick put his arm around her shoulders. "I'll have to drive you by Randy LaChance's house when he gets his Christmas lights up."

"Your friend the police officer?"

"Yeah, he puts all blue lights on his house. All around the windows, the garage, everything. It's so funny when he has the cruiser sitting in the yard." He guided her into the gravel pit entrance.

"Should have brought the .22," he said.

The gravel pit was deserted, and they walked over to the rock where he had set up the cans and sat on it.

"It's too cold to sit still long," Libby said, nestling into his arms.

"I'll try to call you this week. What will they do about Kim's classroom?"

"Get a sub, I guess." Libby hadn't really thought about it.

"We're going to miss our chaperon," Nick said. "I feel like I can't stay at your house long without one."

"Kim's dad is going back tomorrow. He has to work. But her mom's going to stay."

"She'll probably be at the hospital most of the time, though," Nick said glumly.

"When will I see you again, now that hunting season's in full swing?"

"After tonight? Probably at prayer meeting. We'll see. Maybe we can arrange something."

He drove her to church that evening and took her and Stacy home afterward. Libby kissed him at the door and sent

197

him away.

Chapter 38

Permanent Press

Stacy was still awake when Mr. and Mrs. Rutledge came in at nine, and Libby let her get up and kiss her grandparents goodnight.

"You're welcome to stay as long as you want, Mrs. Rutledge," Libby told her guest.

"Thank you, dear, it's a real blessing to have you take us in like this. Paul is heading out early in the morning, but I'd like to stay, at least until Kim leaves the hospital."

"Of course. And I'm sure she would want you to use her car. I'll take Stacy to school with me in the morning, and we'll come by the hospital around three."

***

She rose early on Monday, when the pulp truck passed, and prepared coffee and French toast. Paul and Virginia came downstairs at six o'clock, and Paul brought his luggage.

"Guess I'll go right to the office," he said to his wife. "I'll call you this evening."

Libby left them eating their breakfast and went upstairs to rouse Stacy and help her dress for school. When they saw her grandfather, Stacy was tearful but glad her grandmother was staying.

The days fell into a pattern. Libby adjusted her schedule to give her the extra time needed to meet Stacy and Virginia's needs. She dropped Stacy at the hospital after school each day with her grandmother, then ran errands and shopped. She then went back to visit with Kim for a few minutes and took Stacy home. Supper, laundry, lesson preparation. Nick's call. Virginia's arrival for the night.

Kim gained strength each day, and when Libby went in on Wednesday afternoon, she met her in the hallway.

"Look at you!"

Kim smiled. "Yeah, they're letting me take walks now, as long as I have my friend with me." She nodded toward the IV pole rolling beside her.

"And me," her mother said. "Hi, Libby."

Stacy hugged her mother then took Virigina's hand and walked ahead with her to Kim's hospital room. Libby paced herself with Kim, updating her on school happenings.

The room was filled with flowers. An autumn bouquet from the church vied with a basket of carnations from Kim's students and an arrangement of baby roses from George Franklin.

Nick was faithful in calling Libby each evening. He wasn't able to make it to prayer meeting on Wednesday, and he called apologetically at ten o'clock.

"Did I wake you up?"

"Almost. I was just about to turn the light out."

"Sorry. I had to go to Bingham tonight. Don't ask. Anyway, I'm pretty sure I can go to Westbrook with you on Sunday."

"You'll be tired," Libby said.

"If you wait until I'm rested, it might never happen."

She smiled. "If you're sure, I'll call my folks tomorrow."

"Do it. If I'm too sleepy on Sunday, you can drive. How's Kim?"

"Much better. She said you popped in for a minute yesterday."

"Yes. It was only a minute or two. She still looked fragile

to me."

"Her mother's staying through the weekend, at least," Libby said. "I've enjoyed having her here. She's not at the house much, but of course I feel like I have to keep it clean all the time, so that when she is here she won't think I'm a slob."

Nick laughed. "I don't think anyone would accuse you of being a slob."

"You don't know the real me. I tried to tell you."

"What slobbish sort of things do you do?"

"Oh, leave newspapers and books and assorted paperwork strewn all over the house. Pile stuff on every available flat surface. Clutter."

"Guess I could live with it. Is that the worst thing about you?"

"Hmm...I hate to iron. Are your uniforms permanent press?"

***

Libby was tired by Friday and dragged home later than usual. Mrs. Rutledge had come to the school for Stacy at three, so Libby could stay for a faculty meeting. When she got home, Virginia and Stacy were in the kitchen.

"We've made dinner," Virginia said. "Kim sent us home and told us to take care of you tonight, and I think she's right. You're exhausted. Take your things off, dear, and sit down."

Libby gratefully hung up her jacket and sank into a chair. Virginia's chicken casserole and scalloped potatoes hit the spot.

"I'm planning to visit my parents in Westbrook on Sunday," she said. "Will you and Stacy be all right?"

"I'm sure we will," said Virginia. "If Stacy gets antsy, I'll see if she can't go to the Wilsons' or the Palmers' for a while. But we'll probably spend part of the afternoon here, getting ready for Kim to come home."

"Do they expect her to be discharged Monday?"

"That's her doctor's goal," Virginia said. "I thought, if she does all right for a few days, I might take her and Stacy back to Massachusetts for a week or so."

"I suppose that would be good, if she can travel," Libby said. "It must be difficult for you, staying up here so long."

"I'm afraid it's Paul for whom it's been difficult. I know Stacy would miss school, but she's bright, and if I took her reading and arithmetic with her, I don't think she'd lose that much, do you?"

"I'm sure she could catch up quickly," said Libby.

Chapter 39

Suitor Grilling

Libby slept late on Saturday, turning over and covering her ears when the pulp truck rumbled through. Didn't that man ever take a day off?

When she rose it was rainy, and she thought she saw a slushy snowflake or two. She prepared her clothes for the next day. Nick was picking her up at eight thirty in the morning, so they would get to her parents' house in time to attend church with them.

She prepared everything she would need for school on Monday and checked the cupboards to make sure Virginia and Stacy had all the food they needed, then drilled Stacy on her verse for Sunday school. In the afternoon, she sat down with her Bible and prayer list and lingered over them.

It seemed she was always tired when she got around to praying at night, and she didn't always do justice to the growing list. She prayed earnestly for each of her students and their families, for Kim and Stacy, for the Rutledges and even George Franklin. She prayed for Aiden and thanked God for each circumstance in her life. She spent long minutes praying for Nick, for his future and hers.

He phoned again that evening.

"Wish I could come over," Nick said.

"Better not. Mrs. Rutledge isn't here."

"Can't anyway. Dogs are running deer out near the Sidney

line, and I've got to go out there. Just wanted to check in with you and tell you I'll be there on schedule in the morning. Should I wear a suit?"

"If you do, we'll be ready for church when we get there. But you can bring other clothes to change into if you want. I'm taking jeans."

***

When he arrived she was ready, dressed in her favorite jumper over a turtleneck shirt. Her glossy brown hair was up, knotted on the back of her head. Nick kissed her on the cheek. Stacy was dressed for Sunday school, and Virginia was brushing her hair. Libby said goodbye to them, and Stacy ran to kiss her. Nick lifted the five-year-old in his arms, and she shyly kissed his jaw.

"You have fun today, Mr. Palmer," Stacy said.

"I will, pumpkin. You have fun, too, and make your mommy smile."

"I'll try," Stacy said gravely.

Nick put Libby's bag into the truck for her, and they started out. It was cool but sunny, good driving weather. He headed for the interstate.

The ride was much different than the one to Bangor had been. They talked easily, and the silences were companionable.

"Are you nervous about the test?" she asked.

"Not really. I've been brushing up on the law books. Can't do much else. It's all in God's hands."

"Are you going to be okay with it if you don't get the job?"

"More than okay. I'll be glad."

"You mean that, don't you?"

"Yes, because I've settled that with God. If I don't get it, I wasn't supposed to get it. He'll have something else for me."

Libby said, "But if you do get it—"

"I'll be ecstatic."

She smiled.

Nick reached for her hand. "There's nothing that feels better than knowing God gave you something you really wanted." He glanced sideways at her. "Guess this is where I say you're at the top of my wish list."

She looked out the window, knowing she was blushing, but his open admiration pleased her.

They drove directly to her home church and entered the auditorium as the Sunday school classes were ending and worshipers began filling the pews in the auditorium. Her parents met them in the aisle, embracing Libby warmly.

"You must be Nick," her mother said with approval in her eyes as she extended her hand and looked him over. "I'm Sandra, Libby's mother."

"How do you do, Mrs. Sharpe." His smile was magnetic.

"I'm Richard." Her father smiled and shook Nick's hand. "Call me Dick."

The four of them sat down. "Your brother Ben is coming for lunch," Sandra said to Libby. "I wanted David and the family to come, too, but they couldn't make it."

"That's okay. Next time." Libby thought it would be easier for Nick to meet her family in small doses.

Nick sat circumspectly beside her through the service. He smiled at her occasionally but was attentive to Pastor Carter's sermon.

"I like your church," he said when they walked out afterward.

"Me too," Libby said. "It's different from the one in Waterville, but the spirit is the same."

At the house, she gave Nick a quick tour and left him in the guest room to change his clothes. She went to her old bedroom, where she took down her hair and put on her jeans and long-sleeved, cream knit top. Then she went downstairs to help her mother with dinner.

Ben arrived while they were in the middle of the preparations, and Libby went to greet him with a bear hug. Her father and Nick emerged from the living room, and Libby made the introduction. Dick took the two young men into the living room, giving Sandra and Libby a chance to put the last touches on the meal.

"He's awfully good looking," Sandra remarked, handing her daughter a bowl of mashed squash.

"Guess I forgot to mention that," Libby said.

Her mother smiled. "He's a hero of sorts too."

"Yes. Kim might have died if he hadn't been there."

"He must cut a dashing figure in his uniform."

Libby smiled. "Splendid."

"He has a nice family?"

"Very nice."

"And he's reliable."

"Oh, yes."

"Solvent?"

"Mom, aren't these the questions Daddy usually asks suitors?"

"I thought perhaps we'd spare this one the agony."

"No, it's a thing they have to go through."

Her mother handed her two water glasses. "Your father feels somewhat inadequate in the suitor-grilling department. Feels like he let a bad apple get past him."

Libby knew she meant Aiden. "This one is true and staunch and trustworthy."

"I'll tell your father," Sandra said.

Chapter 40

Hypothetically

Libby went to call the men to the table. Their conversation continued in the dining room. Ben told about his job at the newspaper, and everyone was curious about Nick's work. Mr. Sharpe had never been an outdoorsman and had never met a game warden. Ben had recently taken up archery and told them how he'd been shooting at an indoor range.

Libby was asked about school, and she gave an account of April and Ashley Mitchell's antics as the twins unit progressed. They had broken their own rule and dressed alike one day, frequently switching places to confuse the class.

Libby said, "By the end of the day, I was so mixed up I couldn't even remember which one was supposed to have the gap between her teeth."

When the dishes were done, Ben walked with Nick and Libby around the neighborhood, past their old elementary school and the park where he and his siblings had played as youngsters.

"I guess you can see why I'm so out of my element in the woods," Libby said. "Not a city child, exactly, but a suburban child for sure."

"You turned out okay." Nick took her hand and said to Ben, "So, you played basketball? I played some in high school." The two men kept talking as they walked, and Libby was content to listen. Ben had never liked Aiden, and he'd never deliberately engaged him in conversation. She found the change satisfying.

When they got back to the house, Ben said, "I've got to get rolling. I'm meeting a photographer at four, to cover an anti-pollution rally this afternoon. A bunch of people are trying to stop sludge spreading. It's on the local ballot Tuesday." After saying goodbye to his parents, he pulled Libby aside.

"I could like this guy, Sis."

Libby smiled. "Plan on it."

"Set the date yet?"

"No, but soon, I think."

"Good enough." Ben kissed her on the cheek and turned to shake hands with Nick, who had been standing a few paces back. "Catch you next time, Nick."

Nick watched the tail end of a televised ball game with Dick, and Libby went up to her old room again. She opened the closet and slowly pulled out the wedding dress that had hung there since spring in its protective plastic covering. A waste, she had thought in June. It was non-returnable.

Her mother had said, "Just leave it there, dear. Give it some time before you do anything rash with it."

Libby loved it. She had looked and looked for just the right dress, and she'd finally found it. The style suited her. It was an elegantly simple organza gown with a bouffant skirt. She gazed at it for a long moment then hung it again in the back of the closet and closed the door.

She and Nick had a quiet supper with her parents. She wondered if her father had gotten around to asking the awkward questions yet. Nick seemed at ease.

They headed north at six thirty, but Nick found a spot to pull over before he took the interstate.

"What's wrong?" Libby asked.

"Nothing." He unbuckled his seat belt and slid over next to her and kissed her.

"I enjoyed your family," he said.

"I think they enjoyed you too. I know Ben did. Did Daddy

interrogate you?"

"I don't think so, unless it counts that he asked me if I'd ever been married."

"He asked you that?" Libby was startled.

"He did. I told him no, but that I'm hoping to remedy that soon."

"What did he say?"

"Nothing. Just nodded."

"You and Dad make a pair." Libby laughed.

He kissed her again and said, "Did I tell you I love you today?"

"Not yet."

"I'm slipping already. I do, you know."

"Yes, I can tell."

"Guess I'd better drive."

"Guess you'd better."

They were soon on I-95, and the miles flew as they chatted. He stopped for gas in Augusta.

"Kim's going home tomorrow?" Nick asked when he got back on the highway for the final twenty miles.

"We hope so."

"I'll see if I can come by the house in the evening."

Stacy and Mrs. Rutledge were at home when their journey ended. Stacy had gone to bed, and Virginia was sitting in the dining room writing letters.

"So many people have sent flowers and cards," she said. "Our home church sent money to help with Kim's expenses. Everyone has been so kind. The doctor feels Kim is ready for discharge in the morning. If she does all right this week, I'll take her home next weekend, I think."

Libby made popcorn, and the three ate it and drank apple juice. Virginia washed her hands and went back to her thank-you notes.

"Want to sit for a while?" Libby asked Nick. "We have a chaperon."

He went to the dining room doorway. "Mrs. Rutledge,

would you mind if I sat in the living room with Elizabeth for a little while?"

"Nick," she said, "I don't have a problem with that. I appreciate your courtesy."

He turned back to Libby with a smile and held out his hand. She rose and went with him to the next room and sat down on the couch. He settled beside her with his arm around her and sighed, leaning his head back on the sofa.

"This is nice."

"Yes. No relatives or highways." Libby let her head droop onto his shoulder.

"If a couple decided to get married—just hypothetically, of course," Nick said, "about how long do you think it would take to get ready for the wedding?"

Libby stirred. "Theoretically speaking?"

"Yes."

"It would take a little planning."

"How much?"

"I guess that would depend on what the bride and groom wanted. Big wedding? Small wedding? Bridesmaids? Tuxedoes? A cake, of course. Food for the reception. Invitations. Marriage license. Flowers, church, pastor, photographer ... quite a lot of planning."

"You've ... had some experience on the planning end."

"A bit."

"So, how long?"

"Oh ... a couple of months? Minimum, I mean, for a very small wedding."

Nick kissed the top of her head. "That's not so bad."

"They might want premarital counseling," she said.

"With the pastor?"

"That might be good. Especially if one of them was ... nervous."

"Some pastors might even require it," he said.

Libby turned her head and looked up at him. "The marriage license is good anywhere from three days to three months, I think."

"Three days?" Nick asked. "But the couple couldn't be ready that fast."

"Definitely not. One of them might have a teaching contract. Would she resign?"

"That would be a tough decision. If the groom was being transferred …"

Libby sank back onto his shoulder. "I guess this hypothetical couple has a lot to talk about."

After a moment, he asked, "How would they know when they were ready?"

She sat in silence for a moment, then said, "She'd have to tell him, I guess. Because if he was really being transferred, he would have to know soon, wouldn't he?"

"It would help him a lot. But he wouldn't want to push her if she needed more time." Nick sat forward a little and looked at her intently, then brought his other arm around her and buried his face in her hair. "You always smell good."

Libby turned toward him and moved her hand up the front of his flannel shirt to the collar. He brought his lips to meet hers.

"She's ready," Libby breathed. "That hypothetical girl."

His arms tightened around her. "Will you, Libby? Will you marry me?"

"Yes. But you'll have to help me sort it all out." He held her so tightly she couldn't draw a deep breath. He kissed her hair, her forehead, her cheek and her nose, settling finally on her lips again.

"I love you so much," he said at last. "What needs sorting?"

"My contract. I don't want to let the school down, but … I made that mistake once before. I won't insist on finishing the year. Do you think, if we talked to the pastor, they'd release me at Christmas break?"

"We'll find out," he promised. "I'll call Pastor Mark tomorrow and make an appointment. We'll see him as soon as possible, and he can help us wade through some things. Your job, the counseling, maybe some other stuff. Where do you want the wedding? Here, or in Westbrook?"

"I always thought I'd get married in Westbrook," Libby said, "But now ... I don't know. Your family is all here. Mine could come up. I think I'd really like to have it here. It would be so much easier than trying to make the arrangements long distance while I'm working."

"All right, we'll ask the pastor. If you want to talk to your mother first, go ahead. If she's upset, we can have it down there."

"I don't think anything we decided would upset her, as long as we go through with it."

He squeezed her again. "It's a lock. Nobody changes their mind here."

"I won't," she said, "and I know you won't."

Chapter 41

Wear It for Me

Nick sent Libby to get a calendar and a notebook, and they sat looking at the December page of the calendar.

"Christmas is on a Saturday," he said.

"We don't want to be married Christmas Day, do we?" asked Libby.

He considered. "I don't think so."

"How about the week after?"

"How about the week before?"

She laughed. "School gets out the twenty-second. I think we'd better go with New Year's Day."

"Does it have to be a Saturday?" he asked.

"No. When would be good for you?"

"Sunday. The twenty-sixth. What do you think? Do you need more time off between school and the … wedding? Oh, Libby, it's really real?"

She flung herself at him. "Yes, Nick, yes, it's really real."

A knock on the woodwork at the living room doorway sent her flying backward, away from Nick. He stood up hastily and stammered, "Mrs. Rutledge, I'm sorry, ma'am—we were just—just planning—our wedding."

"Your wedding?" she smiled broadly. "How thrilling! I didn't know."

"Well, ma'am you're—the first to know, I guess." Nick blushed scarlet.

"This is so sweet!" She came into the room and sat down in Kim's rocking chair. "Have you fixed the date?"

"No, ma'am, that's what we were talking about."

Libby was suddenly shy, but she said, "We thought maybe Sunday, December twenty-sixth."

"The day after Christmas." Virginia nodded.

"Yes. Nick might be transferred in January, so we need to have it fairly soon, but not before school breaks for the Christmas vacation."

"Make a list, Elizabeth," Nick said. "We need to go to the jewelry store as soon as we can. Maybe I could meet you there during the lunch hour one day. Do they let you leave school during lunch?"

"I think I could," Libby said, "or right after school."

"Okay, and you'll have to handle the cake and food part. Flowers, license ... what else did you say?"

"Invitations," Libby said, writing in the notebook. "How many bridesmaids and groomsmen do we want?"

"Well, Mike will be my best man. It would be nice if Steve could be here. I don't care how many we have. It's up to you."

"I'd like to have Kim and Jill," said Libby.

Virginia rose. "My dears, I'm going to retire. Please feel free to proceed with your plans. I think this young man is trustworthy." She smiled at Libby.

"Thank you, ma'am." Nick stood up as Mrs. Rutledge went up the stairs, then he sat down again. "Okay, two bridesmaids? I'll get another guy if Steve can't get leave. Drew, maybe, or Randy?"

"Drew Griffin?"

"Sure. We're good friends."

"I didn't realize," Libby said.

"Well, I haven't had time to hang out with him lately, but we've known each other forever."

"Didn't you and Diane ..." she stopped, embarrassed.

"Well, yeah, but that was a long time ago." Nick looked at the list she had started in the notebook. "Does that bother you?"

"I guess not. I just didn't understand how you handled it."

He shook his head. "It wasn't God's will for me. I was a little hurt at first, but ... it's easy to look back now and know for sure she wasn't the right woman for me. It was harder then. But, well, you know. Aiden wasn't right for you."

"Diane didn't smash your heart to smithereens, did she?" Libby asked doubtfully.

"Not really. Our relationship was already pretty much over before she started seeing Drew. And when they got together, it was like dynamite." He laughed. "Drew and I are not at all alike. I don't know why Diane ever liked me in the first place."

"Oh, it's easy to see."

"But she's so outgoing. Almost perky. She used to embarrass me all the time. We'd go to a ball game and she'd scream herself hoarse. Called me a stick in the mud because I wasn't enthusiastic enough. And she loved parties. Not the bad kind, just, you know, being around a lot of people. She and Drew are always throwing parties for the youth group."

Libby said, "I can't see you doing that."

"No way. Diane is best in a room full of people. I think I'm better one-on-one."

"You'd have been miserable," Libby said wonderingly.

"I think so now. But I liked her then. I liked her a lot. Still do, but not that way." He shrugged.

Libby smiled. "Thank you."

"What for?"

"For elucidating that for me. I did wonder about Diane."

"Well, Jill talks too much. So, Mike and one other guy. Tuxedoes?"

"What do you think? Too formal?"

"If you want it, I'll do it."

She couldn't stop smiling. "That's worth a lot. I think I'll save it and call it in on something really important. Wear your gray suit."

"My gray suit?"

"It looks great on you."

"Think so?"

"Know so."

He leaned in and kissed her.

"Guess I'd better go," he said quietly. "Keep your notebook handy and write down anything we need to take care of. I'll set something up with Pastor Wilson tomorrow, and we'll see about getting you a ring at lunch time."

"Nick, I don't need a ring."

"Yes, you do. For me, Libby. I want to buy you one." His look told her it was significant to him. "It can be different from the other one. Was it a diamond?"

"Yes. Square cut, in a gold setting."

"We'll find something different. Something you'll love to wear for the rest of your life."

She put both arms around his neck. "All right."

"Good, because I need to do that. Sort of hanging a sign around your neck for the world to read. You understand?"

"I'm beginning to."

"Anything else that we need to discuss tonight?"

She hesitated. "My dress?"

"Get whatever you want, Elizabeth. You'll be gorgeous, I know."

She leaned back, where she could see his face. "I've already bought one dress, Nick. I'm not sure I want to go through it again. Would it … Do you mind?"

"You still have the dress from … before?"

"Yes." It was a whisper.

He thought for a moment. "Did Aiden pick it out?"

"No, I did. He never saw it."

"But … you bought it for him."

She cocked her head on one side. "I bought it because it was the one I liked best. I really loved it. After he broke up with me, though, I couldn't look at it. Until today."

"Today?"

"At my mother's. It's in the closet in my old room."

"Did you still like it?"

"Yes."

He pulled her down gently against his shoulder again. "Wear it for me, then, if you can get past the associations."

"Are you sure?"

"Yes." He stroked her hair. "I really need to leave."

"Mrs. Rutledge said you're trustworthy."

"I am. That's why I need to leave."

Chapter 42

Great Events

When Libby called home at noon on Monday, Virginia Rutledge answered. Kim was at home, and her mother was coddling her. With permission to leave the school during the lunch hour, Libby met Nick at the jewelry store downtown, and they looked at trays and trays of rings.

"I like that," he said at last, pointing to a gold band with three sapphires and two small diamonds, channel-set along it. The clerk took it out and handed it to Libby. She slid it onto her finger and looked at it critically, then turned a brilliant smile on Nick.

"It's perfect."

She got back to the school just as her students returned to the classroom from recess. Before the last class period, Pastor Wilson came to her classroom door.

"Miss Sharpe," he said quietly, "I've just been on the phone with Nick Palmer, and he asked me to set up an appointment for the two of you."

Libby nodded.

The pastor continued, "I told him I'd be delighted to see you tonight, and he thought he could manage it. He asked me to tell you he'll be at your house at six thirty to pick you up, if that meets with your approval."

"Thank you, Pastor." Libby realized her face was red.

"Congratulations," he said with a smile.

***

Kim was lying on the couch when Libby got home, supported by a mound of pillows. A patchwork quilt was spread over her knees.

Libby hugged her carefully. "How are you doing?"

"Not too bad," Kim said. "I hear great events have transpired while I was in the hospital."

"At least one," Libby admitted.

Kim laughed. "Mom told me this morning. I think it's great."

"It is." Libby laughed, too. "You're going to be my matron of honor."

"Oh, I don't know if I'm up to that."

"It's not for nearly two months. December twenty-sixth, if the church is free that afternoon. We're meeting with Pastor Mark tonight. You'll be healthy by then."

"Well, we'll see. Didn't you say you have a raft of cousins in Belgrade and Oakland?"

Libby scowled. "Second cousins. They're a dime a dozen, but there's only one best friend. I don't want a cousin I barely know as my maid of honor."

"I'd like to, but I don't think I should commit yet."

"Oh, come on, you've got to do it. I was kind of thinking Stacy could be my flower girl too. It will be a small wedding, though. Just you and Jill, I think."

"Who's Nick having?" Kim asked.

"Mike and some as-yet-unknown quantity. His other brother's in the Navy, and they're not sure he can come."

"Mike and Jill? Jill's got to be your matron of honor. Don't make Mike go down the aisle with me!"

"But you're my bestest friend now."

"That's great, but really, Mike's *got* to be the best man, and he and Jill should be together. I'll be your bridesmaid, but I insist on this."

220

Libby smiled. "Well, you've still got some kick. I'll discuss it with my … fiancé." She rolled it off her tongue and grinned at Kim.

"Ooh, this is too exciting," said Kim. "Tell me everything!"

"There's not much to tell yet. We just settled it last night."

"My mother told me." Kim lowered her voice. "She said when she came in here, Nick was kissing you passionately, and it was so romantic she hated to break it up, but she thought it was her duty, so she knocked."

Libby blushed. "It *was* pretty romantic."

"She said if she'd known he'd popped the question, like, twenty seconds before, she'd have waited."

"It's all right. Nick takes our chaperons seriously."

Kim chortled. "He's so funny!"

"He's very earnest."

"He suits you," Kim said.

Libby smiled. "Anyway, you and Jill will have to get together, and we'll discuss your dresses. Nothing too elaborate. The guys are wearing suits. I'm not going to force Nick into a tux, even though he's ready to sacrifice his comfort for me."

"For you, I'll do it."

Chapter 43

Alone Up There

Mrs. Rutledge, Stacy, and Libby took supper into the living room so they could eat with Kim. Libby sat on the floor beside the couch afterward with her notebook in hand, and Kim helped her fill out her list of prenuptial tasks.

At six thirty, Nick rang the doorbell. He had made it home to his parents' house for supper and changed hastily out of his uniform.

"Well, Kim! You look almost healthy," he said, while Libby went for her coat.

"Thank you, Nick." Kim held her hand out to him, and he squeezed it. "Libby tells me I need to buy a new dress soon for an auspicious occasion."

"You'd better believe it. I think you've been rooting for us all along, am I right?"

"I definitely have been."

"I got some news today," he said. "The bullet that hit you came from John Austin's gun."

"He's the man who walked out of the woods that day?"

"Yes. He's still in denial, but he's going to court. It will be a while, though."

Kim grimaced. "I suppose I should be glad that we know now, but I just want it to be over. I keep thinking about what this will do to his family."

Libby stooped to hug her. "You don't need to think about

it, honey. And you know he should be held responsible."

Kim nodded and reached for a tissue.

"I didn't mean to make you sad," Nick said.

"It's all right." Kim managed a watery smile. "I cry at anything now. I'm really okay. You two get out of here."

***

Pastor Wilson met them in his study at the church. Libby sat down, smoothing her skirt nervously, and Nick pulled his chair close to hers and took her hand.

The pastor smiled. "This gives me great joy."

"Well, me, too," Nick said with a grin. They all laughed.

"And the date you wanted was …?"

"December twenty-sixth," Libby said timidly.

He consulted his planning calendar. "A Sunday?"

Nick nodded. "Yes, sir, Sunday afternoon."

"I guess that's all right."

Nick and Libby smiled at each other as the pastor made a memorandum on his calendar.

"You'll do the ceremony, sir?" Nick asked.

"I'd be honored."

Nick glanced at Libby. "Pastor, we need to discuss Elizabeth's contract with the school."

"Oh, boy." Pastor Wilson's face fell. "We've had a terrible time getting a long-term sub for Mrs. Richardson. You wouldn't consider …" He looked anxiously from Nick to Libby and back.

"Well, sir, it's my job," Nick said. "I've put in for a promotion, and if I get it, it would almost certainly mean moving. I won't know until sometime in December."

"I see." The pastor ran his hand through his hair. "I guess we'd better start looking."

"I've been praying for God's will in this," Nick said. "I might not get the position. If I don't, then we'd stay in the area. I think Elizabeth would be willing to finish the school year if

224

that happened."

Libby nodded.

Nick went on, "But we just don't know yet, you see. And if I get it, I either have to pick up and go, or turn it down. I ... don't want to turn it down, sir. I might not have another chance."

"I understand, Nick." The pastor sighed.

Tears were close to the surface for Libby. "I'm sorry. I didn't plan it this way, Pastor. I don't feel very good about breaking my contract, but the alternative would be asking Nick to postpone the wedding for six months, and I—I really don't think I can do that."

Nick stood up and walked to the window. He stood with his back to the room, looking out to where two streetlights illuminated the church parking lot.

"I'll start making inquiries," Pastor Wilson said.

Nick swung around. "Look, I don't want to cause any problems here. I really don't. Six months may not sound like that long, but I've waited a long, long time for this." He paced the three steps to the doorway and swung around, walking back to the window. "I don't want to go up there alone."

Chapter 44

You'll Be Missed

Nick studied the pastor's face. "If I force this on you and then don't get the job, I'll feel pretty foolish, I guess." He sighed. "I'm being selfish, aren't I?"

Pastor Wilson said slowly, "I've known you for several years now, and you've been very faithful. You've encouraged me many times by taking a godly attitude in situations where some people would balk or fume or rebel. I know you try to see things from God's perspective. We've talked about that many times."

Nick's eyes were downcast.

"Let's pray about this situation," the pastor said briskly. "You feel the Lord wants you to get married in seven weeks. Maybe He does. If He does, He'll provide a teacher for us. Either you'll stay here and Libby will continue her job, or He'll send us someone else."

Nick eyed him thoughtfully. "I suppose so. But we might not know until the last minute. I know Libby would feel terrible if we left you without a teacher. And I'd feel terrible because *she* did, and because I'd know I caused you a lot of headaches."

"Let's pray," said the pastor.

Nick sat down and the three of them prayed for God's direction and for the provision of a teacher if one was needed. The pastor prayed last, and he added his plea to God for a blessing on Nick and Libby's union.

"All right," he said to them, "I'll start putting the word out that we need another teacher after Christmas."

"Pastor, would the substitute you have for Kim be suitable?" Libby asked timidly.

"I don't know," the pastor said. "She isn't certified, and I'm afraid she's shaky in math and science."

Libby nodded miserably.

"Don't be all melancholy," said the pastor. "This is a happy occasion. Remember to give thanks in all things!"

"Can you give thanks in losing a teacher?" Libby asked.

Nick said, "We need to. Not just Pastor. If I'm thanking God for giving me a wife, we need to thank Him for taking care of the school's needs, too. Because He'll do something."

The pastor met his gaze. "That's right, Nick. He'll do something. Maybe not what we think would be the ideal solution, but something. Now, we've got the date and we'll see what we can do about the teacher. What else?"

"Well, we wondered about counseling. That is, if you want to…"

"Of course I want to! I refuse to be upset over this teacher thing. God is bigger than that. I usually try to have at least three sessions with engaged couples. When can you two do it? Are Monday nights good?"

"Well, nothing's really good for me in November," said Nick, "but we can try for Mondays. If we have to cancel one or two, I guess we'll have time in December." He looked questioningly at Libby.

"It's fine," she said, and they scheduled the next three Mondays.

Pastor Wilson smiled. "I'm really happy about this. It's been over a year since we had a wedding in the church. It's a wonderful thing."

They left the church at quarter to eight. As soon as they were in his truck, Nick put his arms around Libby.

"Still love me?"

"Of course."

"Even though I threw a tantrum?"

"You did no such thing."

"It felt like it."

"You stood your ground, is all."

"No," said Nick, "I think it's selfishness. I've confessed it to God. Maybe I shouldn't ask for a December wedding."

"No, Nick. I'm not doing that again. I did it before, thinking it was the right thing."

"It was! God didn't want you to marry Aiden, and He used the delay to implement that."

"Well, you don't think He'd use it to separate you and me, do you?" Her voice trembled.

"I sure hope not. Remember what I told you the day Aiden came up here? I said waiting ten months would be a small price to pay. At the time, I meant that. Now … I *am* being selfish. Eight months, instead of two. I should be willing to do that for God's people."

Libby was thoughtful. "Are you saying we should put the wedding off until June?"

"I don't know. Oh, Libby, I don't want to wait that long. This may sound strange, but I'm starting to sympathize with the Black Knight."

"But you would never leave me. You promised." She blinked hard, but a tear spilled over and ran down her cheek.

"No, I'll never do that." He held her close. "This may be some kind of a trial for us, but I truly believe God wants us together."

"How can we know absolutely? I prayed a lot before I accepted Aiden, that God would show me His will, that I'd know what to do. Why didn't He just show me then that Aiden wasn't the right man?"

"I don't know. But I have a deep conviction in my heart that I'm the right man for you. God wants us together. I thought there was no question that it should be before the first of the year. Now I wonder. The school is important too. It involves a lot of our brothers and sisters in Christ."

"I'll stay if you want me to. You can go up there, and I'll come in June."

"No. If you stay, I stay."

"Then, do we go ahead with the wedding?" Libby swallowed hard. "Wouldn't you rather postpone it than give up the job?"

He sighed. "The job isn't a sure thing, anyway. It's a one-in-ten chance."

"Nothing is left to chance with God," Libby said.

"You're right. Let's pray again."

Ten minutes later, a very humble couple stood on the parsonage doorstep.

"Nick, Libby! Come in."

Pastor Wilson took them through the dining room, where Sarah sat at the table preparing Sunday school material, and into the living room beyond.

"Pastor," Nick began, when they were seated, "Libby and I have talked about this and prayed about it." He glanced quickly at Libby, and she squeezed his hand. "We think we should stay here."

"No, Nick, you can't do that," Pastor Wilson said.

"Yes, sir, I can."

The pastor considered. "Don't do anything about it just yet, Nick. Let's see what the Lord brings."

Nick sighed. "I felt guilty after I told you I didn't want to wait. I think God wants me to be willing."

"And you are. I can see that. But don't block off any possibility of getting this promotion. When will you know?"

"I'm supposed to take the test December sixth. It would be sometime after that. Within a week or two, I would hope."

"All right. Proceed with that plan. Be ready to take the test." He looked Nick in the eye. "God can do great things, Nick."

Nick returned his look and nodded.

The pastor put his hand on Nick's shoulder. "I appreciate

you so much, brother. You're not my most vocal parishioner, but what you say counts. If you do go north, you'll be missed."

Chapter 45

If I Could Pick Anyone

Kim, Virginia, and Stacy left for Massachusetts on Friday. Libby's mother drove up to Oakland the next day and joyfully immersed herself in wedding plans with Libby. The guest list began to take shape, and they went to a printer and ordered the invitations. They visited a florist and telephoned a woman Jill Palmer knew who baked wedding cakes.

On Sunday, the Palmer family took advantage of Nick's day off and celebrated the engagement. Justin and Dorothy hosted dinner. Mike, Jill, and their children came, and Libby met Nick's grandmother, Alice Palmer, for the first time.

They all exclaimed over the sapphire ring.

"So unusual," Grandma said. "It accents your lovely blue dress."

"It had to be something unique for Elizabeth," Nick explained.

Jill happily threw herself into the wedding plans. "I'm so glad you don't want tuxedoes, Libby. I've been trying to get Mike to buy a new suit for a year now. This will be the perfect excuse."

Nick had called his brother Steve but hadn't heard yet whether he would be able to attend the wedding.

"Don't you need more than one usher?" Dorothy asked.

"Well, Pastor Wilson said some of the church men will help if we ask them," Libby said, "but they won't have to stand at the front of the church."

"Have someone else single to walk with Kim if Steve can't come," Jill said.

Mike's lips twisted. "Got a single man in your pocket?"

"Well, how about Karl Doherty? He's not bad looking."

Nick held out a hand. "Please, Jill, I don't want to choose my groomsmen based on their looks."

"Good thing," his father put in. "You'd never pick Mike."

"Watch it," Nick said. "Everyone says Mike and I look alike."

They laughed, and Jill asked, "So who were you thinking of?"

Nick shrugged. "Actually, I was thinking about asking Drew."

"Ix-nay," said Mike.

"Why?"

"You know."

"No, I don't know," Nick retorted. "Drew's a good guy."

Jill rolled her eyes. "What, you guys don't like Drew?"

"He's okay," Mike said. "It's just that he—well, you know."

"What?" asked Nick. "Married a girl I used to date? Big deal. How many girls did you date before Jill? They didn't all stay single, did they?"

Jill fixed her husband with a stare and crossed her arms. "This I'd like to hear."

Libby listened to the back-and-forth with amusement but kept still.

"Drew's a friend of mine," Nick insisted, "but if it's going to make you all upset, forget it. I'll ask Randy LaChance."

His mother frowned. "He's not a believer."

Nick sighed. "If I could really pick anyone in the world …"

"Yes?" his mother prompted.

"Well, other than Steve or Dad …"

Justin nodded deferentially. "I'll escort your mother, thank you."

"Who would you pick?" Jill asked.

"Pastor. But I can't. He's doing the ceremony."

"Get Libby's pastor to come up for the ceremony," Mike said. "Pastor Mark can support you, and the church ushers can do the actual ushering."

Nick frowned. "Let's wait a little while on Steve. If there's any way he can be here, I want him."

The talk turned to work. Mike was preparing for the slower season at Agway, bringing in a stock of winter products: rock salt, shovels, splitting mauls, wood splitters, and snow blowers. Justin's job included overseeing the preparation of the state's snowplows for the winter. Nick still had to deal with the frantic hunting season.

"No more accidents this week," he said. "That's good. Some years we have a lot. Some years we don't have any."

"Where did you go tearing off to this morning?" his mother asked.

"Oh, that dog pack was over on the Drummond Road."

"Did you catch up with them?" Justin asked.

"No, I got a distant glimpse. I counted eight, with a big old black one leading them. Looks like a Rottweiler cross. They're picking up strays."

"Are they killing deer?" Jill asked.

"I've seen evidence of three kills. There have probably been more. They were chasing some sheep last week. We've really got to get those dogs."

His mother looked at Libby. "How's Kim? She wasn't in church this morning."

"No, her mother took her and Stacy home yesterday," Libby said. "They've gone to Massachusetts for a week's rest. Mr. Rutledge really wanted them to go down, and the doctor said Kim could travel."

"Is she feeling better?" Jill asked.

"She's doing quite well. She still has some pain, but she's just taking ibuprofen for it now."

"Which means we don't have a chaperon at Libby's house this week," Nick said. "Can we stay here this afternoon and go over the wedding plans, Mom?"

"Of course," Dorothy replied.

"You can come to our house anytime too," Jill offered.

"Well, I haven't been getting in much time with Elizabeth this week," said Nick, "but it's nice to know that when the opportunity arises there's someplace to go."

Chapter 46

The Pack Is Getting Bolder

On Monday evening, Nick met Libby at the church for their counseling session, still in his uniform. Libby didn't mind, but she wished he had a few minutes to relax now and then.

"I'm sweaty," he apologized, kissing her in the church foyer as they went in. "Been chasing that dog pack. I got one of them today."

"Where were they?" Libby asked.

"Out near the airport. They're getting bolder. Ran a deer right onto the runway and took it down on the edge of the road. The airport manager called me. Good thing no planes were trying to land then."

"It's a small airport, isn't it?" Libby asked. "I haven't been out there."

"Yeah, it's mostly private pilots who keep their planes there, and a charter business. No scheduled flights. Hey, isn't one of your cousins a pilot? Does he have a plane there?"

"No, Andrew's gone to work for a small airline, and the family's moved down close to Portland."

"That's right. I heard he and his grandfather sold their farm."

"They did. It was kind of sad, but he sold it to his former in-laws, so they're still welcome to go there and visit anytime they want."

Nick opened the door to Mark Wilson's office, and they

stepped inside.

The pastor greeted them with a smile. "Nick, Libby. Sit down."

"Any word on a teacher yet, sir?" Nick asked.

"Well, I've got a couple of possibilities. The sub in Mrs. Richardson's room might be willing to take a lower class. Thinks she could do better on the third- and fourth-grade level. But I'm hesitant on that arrangement for two full quarters. However, there is another woman who would be excellent. I just have to persuade her that she wants to go back to work."

"Let's pray that God will persuade her," Nick said.

"All right, we will." Pastor Wilson grinned. "She's a grandmother, and she's wonderful with children. She's not certified, but she's very intelligent, and I think she'd do well."

Libby said, "I would give her all my files and plans. I have some fun units made up in advance. If she says yes, I could meet with her and explain what I was going to do."

"I'm sure that would help. I'll go around and see her again this week. She's been out of the work force for a long time, and it would be a big adjustment for her."

"But she's considering it?" Nick asked.

"Yes, she is. As a ministry of six months' duration."

They prayed together, and the pastor opened a notebook and began discussing a variety of topics with the couple. Finances, communication, children. Libby and Nick left his office thoughtfully an hour later. Snowflakes were falling silently.

"Let me take you home," Nick said.

"I've got my car."

"Well, come out to Mom and Dad's for a little while."

"Nick, I've got school tomorrow, and you need to be up at dawn."

He sighed. "You're right."

"Is there anything in particular we need to talk about right now?" she asked.

"No, not really. You're doing great on the wedding

preparations. I don't feel as though I'm doing my share of the work."

"That's okay. Just focus on what you need to do now."

"I'll try."

"Are you studying for the exam, or is it something you can't prepare for?"

"Oh, I'm studying. I've got books in the car on Maine laws, wildlife, forestry, lots of stuff. I cram every time I get a couple minutes."

"I wish I could help you."

"You are."

He kissed her and put her into her Toyota, then waved plaintively at her through the glass.

Chapter 47

One Little Detail

The next week was lonely for Libby. Each afternoon she went home to the empty house. Nick called her most evenings and was able to get to their counseling session. On Friday evening they went together to Mike and Jill's and had a pleasant visit with them.

The third week of November, Libby began her Thanksgiving theme unit. She read stories of the Mayflower children to her students, and they acted out the landing of the Pilgrims and the first Thanksgiving. They did myriad art projects and cut up apples for a lesson in fractions, then ate their manipulatives.

She planned her December unit with a Christmas theme for the three weeks of school and looked ahead to what she could suggest for the new teacher. Water, perhaps, for January. That could incorporate various forms of weather, study of the oceans, simple science experiments, literature that touched on the sea, and mapping in social studies.

Kim had returned to her classroom but was still weak. The substitute was vanquished, to the junior high students' delight. The other teachers volunteered to take over Kim's extra duties for her.

Nick was able to spend an evening at the farmhouse, but he was so tired he nearly dozed off on the sofa. Libby got him a cup of coffee. She had planned to address the invitations with him that night, but he was obviously exhausted, so she didn't say anything about it. She did show him one of the invitations that had arrived that day, with their names officially printed together in raised script. He smiled as he looked at it.

"Can't change anything now," he said.

He rallied for half an hour and approved Libby's menu for the reception. The church social committee would prepare the food, and Kim's class had volunteered to decorate the gymnasium. Stacy modeled the red velvet dress she would wear as flower girl. Nick's eyelids began to droop again.

"I hate to say it," Libby said regretfully, "but you might do better to go home and get all the sleep you can. Tomorrow's another long day for you."

He staggered to his feet and walked with her to the kitchen. "I just wish we had more time together. When I'm conscious, that is. We're supposed to be talking a lot and getting to know each other better, but I don't think we've made much progress this week."

The Monday evening counseling session had been canceled that week because Nick was called to the southern end of his territory and didn't make it back in time. He had missed prayer meeting on Wednesday but kept in touch with Libby by means of texts and frustratingly brief phone calls.

Meanwhile, Libby had at last phoned an aunt in Belgrade and obtained addresses so she could invite extended family members to the wedding.

Kim and Stacy had stayed behind them in the living room, and in the kitchen Nick drew Libby into his arms. "Sunday," he said. "I'll see you Sunday."

He was at Sunday school looking more rested, and they went to his parents' house for dinner. They walked through the new snow in the pasture behind the Palmers' house that afternoon, then sat snugly before the fireplace with Nick's parents, making plans and holding hands.

"One more week," he said. "I love hunting season, but this year I'll be glad when it's over."

On Monday, he made it to the second counseling session. The pastor was ready with questions and discussion topics that took them into deep emotional waters. Libby felt her love for Nick strengthening as they pledged to meet each challenge together.

Thanksgiving was upon them, and Libby was going home for the weekend. She had planned to leave early Wednesday, but the school directors had decided to use that planned vacation day as a makeup day for one of those lost during the power outage. She drove to Westbrook Wednesday evening, arriving at her parents' home late and tired.

She enjoyed seeing her brothers and David's family. The talk on Thursday and Friday centered on her upcoming wedding. By Saturday morning, she was ready to go back to Oakland. It was the last day of hunting season, and Nick would have three days off, beginning Sunday.

In her old bedroom, Libby opened the closet door. When she unzipped the protective bag that held her wedding gown, the dress seemed more beautiful than ever. She laid it carefully over her arm and carried it downstairs.

"I'm taking this back with me," she told her parents. Her father took it from her and carried it to her car, hanging it in the back seat and spreading the skirt out along the seat in its plastic cover.

"Four weeks," her mother said, hugging her. "Think it will all come together?"

"I'm not going to get upset if something's not perfect," Libby said. "Pray for Nick when he takes the test, okay? He really wants that job, and the test is a big part of it."

He didn't call that evening, but he arrived at the house at nine fifteen Sunday morning. They got to the church early for Sunday school and sat in his pickup in the parking lot.

"What will you do with your three days off?" Libby asked.

"Well, this one I intend to spend with you, and to stay awake." He laughed. "I guess tomorrow I'll do some errands. Is there anything I should be doing for the wedding?"

"I think it's under control," Libby said.

"Where are we going after?"

"I—don't know. We haven't talked about where we'll live or anything."

"I'm hoping we're going north," Nick said. "We might end up with no place to live, I guess. Should we look into a rental or something?"

"I don't know." Libby frowned. "If we end up staying here, we'll need something."

Nick took a deep breath, and Libby saw excitement in his eyes. "I talked to my supervisor last night. There are only eight of us taking the test now. He thinks that if all else is equal, only two of them are serious competition for me."

"Really?" Libby was gleeful, almost giddy.

"Yeah, well, I know one guy. He's forty, and he's been a warden for about twenty years. He's almost a legend, and I don't know why he never made supervisor before this. Maybe he didn't want to move. Anyway, I think he's the top candidate."

Libby sobered. "So, you still don't think you'll get it?"

Nick looked out the side window toward the school classrooms. "I just don't know. Keep praying."

"Maybe we *should* look for a place to live," she said. "Kim and Stacy are going to Massachusetts for the Christmas vacation. Do you want me to ask her if we could stay at the house while she's gone?"

"That's our honeymoon time," Nick said.

"Well, I wasn't sure we were going anywhere ..." she looked at him helplessly.

"Oh, boy, pretty stupid of me," he said.

"No, you've just been so busy. I didn't want to bother you."

He shook his head, smiling. "Libby, the honeymoon is one little detail I don't want to forget."

Cars were pulling into the parking lot. Nick reach to open his door.

"Look, let's go out for lunch today and talk about it, okay?"

Chapter 48

The Back of Beyond

Nick picked Libby up for their final counseling session on Monday evening. As he drove toward the church, he reported to her that the arrangements for their wedding trip were complete.

"Fast work," she said.

"Well, when I have the time and the incentive, I can accomplish a lot," he replied. With the influence of his supervisor, he had secured the use of a remote but winterized lakeside cabin owned by the Fish and Wildlife Department. Nick's friend Randy had offered the loan of his snowmobile for the week.

"Randy thinks this is hysterically funny."

"Why?" Libby asked.

"He says we should be going to Bermuda or someplace warm, especially if we might be living in Siberia for the next few years."

"Siberia, huh?"

"That's what he called it. Are you sure—"

"We talked about that," Libby said. "I'm sure. If you have the chance to live in the Great North Woods, I want to be there with you."

The pastor had news of the replacement teacher for them that evening.

"She's decided she's willing to do it," he told them with

evident relief. "I know she'll do well. And she understands that if you're not moving out of the area she won't be called upon."

"Great," said Libby. "Can I meet with her? Would she like to visit the classroom?"

"Well, perhaps," the pastor said. "I'll ask her about it. Maybe we can arrange something."

"I'd really like to help her all I can."

Pastor Wilson smiled. "I'm sure that's true. She says she's starting to look forward to it. Her husband wasn't too keen at first."

Libby hadn't thought about there being a husband involved. "He doesn't want her to work?"

"Well, he's used to having her at home, but their children are all gone now, and he's agreed it might be a blessing for them. God uses things in ways we can't foresee. And speaking of God's timing, there's something else that might interest you. The Boudreaus are going to Florida right after Christmas and coming back in March. They're interested in having someone reliable house-sit for them."

"You mean, us?" Nick asked.

"Well, if you get the promotion, you'll need a place to stay while you get ready, won't you?"

"Yes, I guess we will. We've talked about looking for a rental, but we don't want to put a deposit on something and then find out we're leaving."

"Well, this would give you a breathing spell," Mr. Wilson said. "If you don't get the job, you can stay on at Boudreaus' for a couple of months and look for a house or an apartment. If you do get it, you can stay there a week or two, whatever you need. Clive Boudreau said they'd appreciate any time you'd spend there. They worry about break-ins."

"That sounds pretty good for us," Nick admitted, looking expectantly at Libby.

"Very good," she agreed.

The week flew. Nick came most evenings to the house, relaxed and contented to sit with Libby and Kim, reading stories to Stacy, eating cookies, playing word games, and reading student papers. He especially enjoyed reviewing Joey's work.

On Sunday evening, the night before the test, he and Libby prayed earnestly together for the accomplishment of God's will. Nick spent the entire day Monday in Augusta and showed up on Libby's doorstep at five o'clock.

"You're just in time for supper," Kim said, reaching for an extra plate. "Good thing I made too much spaghetti."

"How'd it go?" Libby asked, as he took off his snowy boots on the mat.

"Not bad. Seven of us were there."

"Another man dropped out?"

"Actually, it was a woman. There was some talk of them promoting her as the first female warden supervisor. There aren't any quotas or anything, but once in a while someone says something about how heavily male the department is. But she didn't show up today, so she's out of the running."

"Any indication of when you'll get the results?"

He shook his head. He had brought in his Maine atlas and showed her and Kim where the supervisor's house was located in the northwest area of the state.

"You have to go up 201 to Jackman and cross into Quebec to get there," he said, tracing the roadway north with his index finger. "Past St. Juste, to Daquaam. You cross back into Maine at the checkpoint, here. There's a gate. The house is right in here, on the Daquaam River."

Kim stared at the map. "Wow! That's the back of beyond."

"Yeah," Nick said happily.

"Tell me again why you volunteered for this alienation?" Kim asked.

"It'll be great," he said. "If we go."

Kim considered for a moment. "I think you and Libby will be content. It's not for me, but I would like to come and visit you for a day or two sometime."

"Of course," Libby said. "You have to. We'll want some

link with civilization."

"Maybe Stacy and I can mush in supplies on a dogsled for you." Kim laughed.

"Will you have a dogsled, Aunt Libby?" Stacy asked, her china blue eyes large.

"No, honey. Your mommy's teasing. But we will want you to visit us."

"And if we don't move north, we'll still want you to come see us," Nick added. "We might stay right here."

"With us?" Stacy almost squealed.

"Well, not in this house."

"Oh." Stacy drooped.

"But close by," he assured her, "and at the same church. That's if I don't get the job up north."

He lingered that evening, savoring Libby's company. Finally she told him she and Kim needed to sleep, and he sighed and got up, reaching for his jacket.

"Three weeks," she said, to placate him.

"Twenty days," he corrected.

Chapter 49

A New Experience

It was Wednesday, the fifteenth, and still Libby had not met the replacement teacher. The pastor wasn't in his office. She decided to walk over to the parsonage after school to see if he was home. The students had gone, and her duties for the day were done.

As she crossed the parking lot, Nick's black Explorer with the state seal on the door entered the parking lot. He saw her and drove up close to her, stopping the vehicle in the middle of the lot.

"Libby! I'm glad I caught you!" He jumped out and embraced her fiercely.

"What is it?" she asked breathlessly, looking over her shoulder. Mrs. Pelkey, the school secretary, smiled indulgently and moved toward her car.

"The test, Libby, the job, everything. I got it! We're going to Daquaam."

Libby gasped with joy. "Oh, Nick, I'm so happy!" She threw her arms around him, and he squeezed her again, laughing and lifting her off the pavement.

"Let's go tell Pastor Wilson," he said. "He'll need to tell the new teacher."

"I was just going to talk to him about that. I still haven't met her, and school ends next week."

They walked hand in hand to the parsonage, and Nick rang

the doorbell. Sarah admitted them and called her husband in from his study.

"Pastor, I got the job." Nick grinned, unable to conceal his excitement.

"Well, I'm pleased." Pastor Wilson grasped Nick's hand heartily. "God is good, isn't He?"

Nick nodded.

"So, the Great North Woods adventure begins in eleven days," Sarah said with a smile.

"Well, not quite that soon," Nick said. "They're sending me to the Criminal Justice Academy for special training for two weeks in January. I'm supposed to report to my new post February first."

Libby did some calculating. "So we can stay at the Boudreaus' house through January?"

"I guess so," Nick said. "It will give us time to plan and pack. I'll commute to the academy from there."

"It's not very far, is it?" Libby asked.

"No, only ten miles or so from Boudreaus'."

"Well, it seems the Lord has provided everything you need," the pastor said, and Libby knew he was genuinely happy for them.

"There's one thing," she said. "I haven't met the new teacher yet."

"Oh, yes, you're right," Mr. Wilson said. "I had thought we'd wait until you knew for sure. Now is the time to call her, I guess. Why don't you two sit down, and I'll give her a buzz. Maybe she could come over right now."

"Oh, that's not necessary," said Libby. "Anytime—"

"No, no," said the pastor. "I told her I'd let her know as soon as possible. Sit down."

Sarah took their jackets and served Nick and Libby milk and brownies. She kept them talking about their future plans until her husband came back to the kitchen.

"It's all set," he said. "She'll be here in about ten minutes."

He sat down and took a brownie, and Sarah brought him a glass of milk.

"You've been so mysterious about her," Libby said. "Are you sure she wants to do this?"

"Positive," he replied. "She was quite excited when I told her. Now, Nick, you'll want to call Clive Boudreau and tell him what your plans are. I'm sure they'll be pleased that you're going to stay at the house for a month."

The conversation flowed until the doorbell rang and Sarah jumped up to open the door. They all turned expectantly.

"Mom?" Nick stared at her.

"Yes, here I am," Dorothy said.

"You're not—" he broke off, staring at his mother. "You are, aren't you?"

She advanced and put her arms around him. "Yes, I am. It will be a new experience."

"Mom, you can't do this. Six months—"

"Oh, Mrs. Palmer," Libby said. "We had no idea. It's such a big job."

"I expect I can handle it."

"But Mom," Nick protested. "You can't!"

"I can," she said firmly. "For the Lord, and for my son." She laughed. "I'm going to see more of my grandson Joey, too."

"And Dad approves of this?" Nick eyed her skeptically.

"He does now. When I first broached the subject, he was a little leery, but after we'd spent about a week praying about it, the idea sort of grew on him. Don't worry about us. For the first time in over thirty years, we won't have any children living at home. I won't have as much cooking and laundry to do. Besides," she said with a smile, "I'll earn a little pocket money."

Chapter 50

Deerly Beloved

At four o'clock on Christmas Day, the wedding party gathered at the church auditorium for the wedding rehearsal. Steve Palmer had flown in to Bangor the day before, and Nick had picked him up at the airport. His sisters had driven up with their families. Libby had spent Christmas Eve with her family in Westbrook, and her parents had driven up with her Saturday morning. Her brothers would come for the day Sunday.

"Well, I think this has been the easiest wedding rehearsal I've ever conducted," Pastor Wilson said when they felt they had practiced enough. "A small wedding party, all Christians. Nobody stuck in traffic or sick at the last minute, no bickering over the music. It's gone very smoothly."

"You sound as though you don't enjoy weddings," Nick said with a laugh. He put his arm around Libby's waist, and she leaned against him. He wore his uniform, having worked most of the day so others could have the holiday off before he took two weeks' vacation for his honeymoon.

"Oh, it's not usually the wedding," said the pastor. "It's the rehearsal. The wedding usually goes off without a hitch. Although there was one time when the groom couldn't find the ring."

"That wasn't the worst time," Sarah said. "Remember the one in our last church, sweetheart, where the groom stormed out halfway through the rehearsal?"

"Well, yes, there is that," the pastor said gravely. "The worst wedding experience we've ever had, I guess."

"Let's go eat supper," said Mike, and everyone agreed, picking up coats, mittens and purses from where they had left them on the pews.

The barking and baying of dogs outside the church interrupted their preparations. Nick looked toward the windows on the right side of the church where he and Libby usually sat, but the glass was textured and he couldn't see out.

"Sounds like they're after something," Mike said.

Libby listened. The barking grew closer, and she heard snarling and snapping.

Steve cocked his head to one side. "Sounds like a dog fight."

Nick strode to the nearest window and threw it open. "Oh, man!"

As he said it, the stained glass window near the front on that side shattered, and pieces of the blue and purple Sea of Galilee flew into the room, showering the first three pews with shards of glass. A whitetail buck thudded onto the floor in front of the first pew.

It lay stunned for half a second, then struggled to get up. Blood spurted from a gash just behind its front leg. It gained its footing and tossed its head, regal antlers menacing the staring people.

Everyone stepped back, away from the frightened deer. Kim edged into the nearest pew, pushing Stacy before her.

Nick ran to the broken window. Dogs outside it growled and leaped at the jagged opening. He grabbed a hymnbook and swung at them, hitting one soundly on the nose. It retreated, whimpering, but another lunged up, halfway into the auditorium, its shaggy black head and forelegs through the window. It hung there, snarling.

"Nicky, the glass," Mike shouted. "Be careful!"

The deer turned toward the window, lowering its head and snorting.

Nick tried to push the large dog out the window, but it snapped viciously at his arm. He pulled his revolver and put it to the dog's head.

Libby gasped and turned away. The report of the pistol was louder than she had expected, and Stacy put her hands to her ears belatedly. The dog pack ran away yelping. When Libby looked at Nick, he was lifting the black dog and heaving it out the broken window.

"What about the deer?" Pastor Wilson asked. He was standing closest to it. It stood terrified, rolling its eyes. Blood streamed down its front leg, pooling on the carpet.

"Everybody stay back," Nick said. He walked slowly toward the animal, over the broken glass. "His leg doesn't seem to be broken."

"You got a tranquilizer gun?" Steve asked.

Nick shook his head. "It would take an hour to get one here." He looked around. "What a mess." The deer stood still, eyeing him.

"It's bleeding all over the rug," Jill said. "What can we do?"

"Maybe we can chase it out the door," Mike suggested.

Mark Wilson looked to Nick. "Do you think it will be all right if it gets out of here?"

"Doubtful. Not with that dog pack hanging around. It really needs veterinary attention."

"Well, it will never let us carry it out of here alive," Mike said. "Maybe you should shoot it."

"No!" Jill cried.

Mike said, "Well, then at least we could get it out of the auditorium."

"Whatever you think, Nick," said the pastor, watching the deer uneasily.

Nick hesitated. The buck lowered its head and took a threatening step toward him.

Chapter 51

Our Last Date

"Can you get something to tie it with? Rope or cloth, anything?" Nick asked.

"I'll get something." Sarah hurried toward the basement stairs.

"Libby, hand me my jacket." Nick extended his hand slowly, keeping both eyes on the buck.

Libby went quickly to where he had dropped his coat on the floor. She picked it up and started toward him, but the deer swung toward her and snorted.

"Toss it," said Nick.

She threw it toward him, and Nick caught it. The deer backed up a step and lowered its head, weaving slightly with its antlers pointed at Nick.

"All right, Pastor, Mike, Steve," Nick said quietly. "Let's try to corner him. I want to wrestle him down and look at the wound. If he's going to be okay, we can have him transported to the game park until he recovers. If he needs veterinary attention, we can take him over to the animal hospital."

The women stayed in the shelter of the pews as the men advanced slowly, encircling the deer.

"He's gonna make a break for it," Mike said, as the buck pawed the rug threateningly and shook his antlers at them.

Nick opened his jacket and held it out before him.

"You only get one chance," Steve said.

As the deer flexed to spring, Nick flung the jacket around its head, and his brothers and the pastor leaped in to help take the animal to the floor. It struggled and kicked, but Steve sat on its neck. Nick grabbed its flailing foreleg and extended it, quickly examining the wound.

Sarah came puffing into the auditorium, with a ball of strong twine in her hands. "Is this all right?"

Libby's father took it from her and carried it to Nick.

"It might hold, if you used enough strands," he said.

Mike produced a pocketknife to cut lengths of twine, and the men worked feverishly to restrain the deer. They tied all four legs together.

"Hurry up," Steve gasped, as the deer renewed its struggles.

"All right!" Nick and the others stood up, and Steve pulled the jacket free.

The deer lay defeated, breathing fast, white showing at the edges of its terrified eyes.

"Now I need to phone a vet and Tom Hatfield," Nick said, panting. "I don't think the wound is that bad, but the dogs would follow the blood trail and run him down in no time if we let him loose."

"You can use the phone in my study," Mark said.

Nick called over his shoulder, "Mike, if you can get a rag, try to stop the bleeding.

"I don't want to get near that critter again. His legs may be tied, but he's still dangerous."

"I'll find something," Jill said, and she left the room.

Libby's father surveyed the damage to the stained glass window. "We'll have to hang something over that hole."

Half an hour later, Sarah called the restaurant and canceled the rehearsal dinner.

"Hey, everybody, they're going to pack up the meal and deliver it here, since you have to pay for it anyway," she announced.

A cheer went up from the wedding party and family

members.

The pastor was still vacuuming the church rug for slivers of glass. Nick had let his brothers help him and Tom lift the two-hundred-pound deer and carry it out to the back of Tom's truck, and now Mike and Steve were hanging a sheet of clear plastic over the window frame and trying to secure it. Dick Sharpe was handing them tape and tacks.

Nick filled out paperwork while Tom waited to drive the deer to the animal hospital for treatment.

"The vet says he'll keep him in a large dog pen overnight." Nick handed Tom the forms.

"I'll go over tomorrow and arrange for its release," Tom offered.

Nick had thrown the dead dog into the back of Mike's pickup on some feed sacks. It had no collar, and he had no hope of identifying its erstwhile owner. He took the rags Sarah brought from the cleaning closet and went to join the pastor in scrubbing the bloody rug.

Sarah took Jill and Kim with her to the parsonage to accept the restaurant's delivery and set out the food. When supper was ready, the men stopped their work and washed up. They went over to the parsonage kitchen long enough to eat then they returned to the church.

It was past ten o'clock before they decided they'd cleaned the carpet as well as they could. It was still wet, and only time would tell if the stain would show. The pastor set up a fan nearby to dry it faster. The window was covered with a double layer of plastic. Nick was the only one with an injury, a slight cut on his forearm. Sarah had bandaged it and declared it was not serious.

"Well, I guess we have a new rehearsal experience to add to our collection," Pastor Wilson sighed. "Nick, for a quiet bachelor, you're going out with a real bang."

***

"Fourteen hours," Nick said when he dropped Libby off at midnight. They had lingered at the pastor's house. Kim had taken Stacy home earlier, and Libby's parents, who were staying at the farmhouse that night, had retired. Kim had left the kitchen light on for her roommate.

Libby took off her jacket. "We should thank God for the deer jumping through the window, but I can't see why He let that happen."

"It probably saw trees reflected in the glass and thought it could go through there, like when a bird flies into a window," Nick said.

She nodded. "I'm glad it survived. Thanks for making sure that happened."

Nick glanced at his watch. "Hey, it's 12:05 a.m. It's our wedding day."

Libby smiled at him. "You'd better go home and sleep."

"I will. Can I pick you up for Sunday school?"

"Why don't I just ride in with my folks?"

"All right, but you'd better save me a seat," Nick said.

"Absolutely."

He bent his head to kiss her, and Libby's left hand slid in under his right arm, and her right hand went up to the back of his neck. He held her securely for a few seconds.

"This is the last time I'm going to send you away," Libby said.

He nodded soberly. "Our last date."

"Dates with you can be hazardous, Nick Palmer."

"Got your courage up for tomorrow?" he asked softly.

"It's going to be easy," she said with conviction. "I never wanted anything so much. How about you? Any qualms tonight?"

"None." He stroked her glossy hair.

Libby rested her head on his shoulder for a long moment, then nudged him toward the door. "Thirteen hours and forty-five minutes," she said.

"I'll be there."

THE END

If you missed the rest of the series, please enjoy an excerpt from Book One in the Mainely Romance Series, *She Gets July*:

Rebecca froze when she spotted a postcard nestled innocuously between the phone bill and an L.L. Bean catalog. An eagerness she would have denied made her fingers shake as she picked it out of the day's handful of mail, and she read it with bittersweet satisfaction. Rob was faithful, even though she had released him from all commitment three years ago.

Dear Rebecca, I've checked things out and turned on the water and electricity. Any time you want to use the cottage, it's ready for you. RW

She stared at the neat, backward-slanted printing he had developed in grammar school, and tears came to her eyes. She dropped the postcard to the table and went to her bedroom to change out of her nursing uniform, determined to put Rob Wallace out of her mind.

She fixed herself a sketchy supper and carried it to the living room, where she ate it while watching the local news. When she took her dishes to the sink, she realized she was avoiding the table because she didn't want to see the postcard again, and she didn't want to think about Rob.

But the cottage was still an important part of her life, even if Rob wasn't. She picked up the card and flipped it over to examine the address side. It was the plain manila card sold in the post office, not the scenic kind, with lovely Maine vistas enticing you to get away for the weekend in Vacationland.

That was just what she would do. The cottage was hers for the rest of May, and she would go up this weekend. The ice had barely gone out of the lake, and the water would still be too cold for swimming, but she could sit on the dock in the late spring sun and have a fire in the stone fireplace in the chilly evenings. And she could get out and walk for miles on the dirt roads near the lake, satisfying her latent longings for the country.

Of course, there would be reminders of Rob everywhere. She didn't need any photos to see him, even after all this time. In her mind's eye, he was there, bent over the postcard with the pen in his left hand, frowning in concentration over the address, his brown eyes placid and his chestnut hair fluffy and tousled.

Her eyes stung, and she blinked hard. It was worth the painful memories, to get away from Portland for a couple of days and blow the cobwebs from her brain.

She wavered, looking down again at the words he had written—when? Yesterday? The day before? The postmark said May 4. Saturday, two days ago.

She hadn't seen him in more than three years. They'd talked on the phone a couple of times, briefly. It was business only, to tie up loose ends concerning the cottage. He never tried to see her when she drove an hour to the north to use it. But the postcards had come every spring. *Rebecca, the cottage is ready.*

〈⌳〉

Rob sat at his computer, fine-tuning an elevation for a new elementary school. In a few more hours, he'd be done with the project, but he didn't really want to be finished. Between projects, his mind drifted too much, and he didn't want that right now.

He'd been out to the cottage Saturday, to check on things and make sure it was ready for Rebecca. It was May, and she'd be going there soon. May was hers, then he would move to the lake for a month.

On the last day of June, he would pack up all his things and move from the lakeside, back to his parents' home, so she could claim the cottage for the month of July. And on the first day of August, he would move back to the lake. It happened every year. People thought it was strange. Fine, let them think that.

His phone rang, and he picked it up.

"Hi, honey. Ready for lunch?"

Rob winced, but he was too polite to tell Brittany how uncomfortable her syrupy greeting made him. "Uh, sure. I'll meet you downstairs in a couple of minutes." He saved the computer file and stood.

"The princess beckons?" Eric, at the next desk, was a good friend, but he enjoyed needling Rob. "The chains of slavery are tightening."

Rob scowled at him. "What do you suppose your wife would say if she heard you talking like that?"

Eric grinned. "Leah would say, 'That's right. Eric's been my slave for seven years.' And she'd be right."

"You've only been married five." Rob reached for his jacket.

"Trust me, friend, it starts long before the wedding. Look at you, scrambling every day at noon."

"Twice a week," Rob said. "I told her I can't do lunch more than that."

"Oh, so you're in control, not Brittany. I'll bet you're Johnny-on-the-spot Friday nights, too. Next thing you know, she'll have you picking her up for work every day, even though it's miles out of your way. You might as well marry her now."

That hit home. Brittany had suggested he pick her up in the morning, but Rob had begged off. He shrugged. "Hey, it's not that serious."

Eric nodded doubtfully. "Right. You've been dating how long?"

"Just a couple of months."

"Mm-hmm. Two months."

"Or three. I forget."

"Tell me she hasn't been hinting for a diamond."

Rob frowned. "It's pretty early for that, don't you think?"

"So? Talk isn't enough for a woman like Brittany. If you don't cough up a tangible token of your adoration—preferably a ring—pretty soon, she'll make you miserable."

"Did Leah do that to you?"

"Well, no, but Leah's nothing like Brittany. Not her type at all."

Rob headed for the elevator shaking his head. He wasn't ready to make things exclusive with Brittany, let alone permanent, but he wasn't about to admit it when Eric was implying that marriage was a deathtrap. Eric made no secret of his opinion that Brittany was the wrong choice for Rob, and he couldn't resist ribbing him every chance he got.

Maybe Eric was right. Brittany was a bit of a clinging vine. She definitely wanted to move things along faster than Rob did. If Eric wasn't so cynical, maybe Rob could talk to him seriously about the relationship. But he knew what Eric would say. *Run, do not walk.*

About the author

Susan Page Davis is the author of more than one hundred published novels. She's a two-time winner of the Inspirational Readers' Choice Award and three Will Rogers Medallions, and also a winner of the Carol Award and a finalist in the WILLA Literary Awards and Selah Awards. A Maine native, she now lives in Kentucky. Visit her website at: https://susanpagedavis.com, where you can see all her books, sign up for her occasional newsletter, and read fun features on her "Freebies" tab. If you liked this book, please consider writing a review and posting it on Amazon, Goodreads, or the venue of your choice.

Find Susan at:

Website:
https://susanpagedavis.com
Amazon:
https://www.amazon.com/Susan-Page-Davis/e/B001IR1CGA
BookBub:
https://www.bookbub.com/authors/susan-page-davis
Twitter:
@SusanPageDavis
Facebook:
https://www.facebook.com/susanpagedavisauthor
BookCave:
https://mybookcave.com/profile/susan-page-davis/
Goodreads:
https://www.goodreads.com/author/show/255473.Susan_Page_Davis

And subscribe to her newsletter to receive a free short story:

https://madmimi.com/signups/118177/join

More of Susan's Novels you might enjoy:

Contemporary Romances:

Mainely Romance series:
She Gets July
Off the Record
The Charm Bracelet
Trail To Justice
Alaska Weddings Series:
Always Ready
Fire and Ice
Polar Opposites
Love Comes to the Castle
Revolution at Barncastle Inn
Short and Sweet: 13 Sweet, Romantic Stories

Mystery and Romantic Suspense:

True Blue Mysteries:
Blue Plate Special
Ice Cold Blue
Persian Blue Puzzle
Scream Blue Murder
Skirmish Cove Mysteries
Cliffhanger
The Plot Thickens
Backstory
The Maine Justice series:
The Priority Unit
Fort Point
Found Art
Heartbreaker Hero
The House Next Door
The Labor Day Challenge
Ransom of the Heart

The Saboteur

The Frasier Island Series:
  Frasier Island
  Finding Marie
  Inside Story
Breaking News
Just Cause
You Shouldn't Have
Hearts in the Crosshairs
What a Picture's Worth
The Mainely Mysteries Series (coauthored by Susan's daughter, Megan Elaine Davis):
  Homicide at Blue Heron Lake
  Treasure at Blue Heron Lake
  Impostors at Blue Heron Lake
Tearoom Mysteries (from Guideposts, written by several authors):
  Tearoom for Two
  Trouble Brewing
  Steeped in Secrets
  Beneath the Surface
  Tea and Promises
  Tea Leaves and Legacies

Also from Guideposts, selected books by Susan appear in the Patchwork Mysteries, Mysteries of Mary's Bookshop, Miracles of Marble Cove, Secrets of the Blue Hill Library, and Mysteries of Silver Peak series.

Historical novels:

Homeward Trails Series:
  The Rancher's Legacy
  The Corporal's Codebook
  The Sister's Search
The Outlaw Takes a Bride (western)
Counterfeit Captive
Almost Arizona

River Rest (set in 1918)
The Crimson Cipher (set in 1915)
Mrs. Mayberry Meets Her Match
Hearts of Oak Series (Co-authored with Susan's son James S. Davis, set in the 1850s):
    The Seafaring Women of the Vera B.
    The Scottish Lass
The Ladies' Shooting Club Series (westerns):
    The Sheriff's Surrender
    The Gunsmith's Gallantry
    The Blacksmith's Bravery
Captive Trail (western)
Cowgirl Trail (western)
Hearts in Pursuit (western novella)
Christmas Next Door
Echo Canyon
The Prairie Dreams series (set in the 1850s):
    The Lady's Maid
    Lady Anne's Quest
    A Lady in the Making
Maine Brides series (set in 1720, 1820, and 1895):
    The Prisoner's Wife
    The Castaway's Bride
    The Lumberjack's Lady
Seven Brides for Seven Texans
Seven Brides for Seven Texas Rangers
White Mountain Brides series (set in 1690's in New Hampshire)
Wyoming Brides series (set in 1850s):
    Protecting Amy
    The Oregon Escort
    Wyoming Hoofbeats
The Island Bride (set in the 1850s)

And many more. **See all of her books** at
https://susanpagedavis.com.

www.ingramcontent.com/pod-product-compliance
Lightning Source LLC
Chambersburg PA
CBHW070728280626
47159CB00023B/2878